BIGFOOT BROTHERS

CHRIS BOSSY

Pudgy Press LLC

Bigfoot Brothers is a work of fiction. All of the characters, organizations, and events portrayed in this novel are either products of the author's imagination or are used fictitiously.

Copyright © 2022 by Chris Bossy

Excerpt from *Gold Diggers: A Sasquatch Attack Survival Story* by Chris Bossy. Copyright © 2022 by Chris Bossy

All rights reserved. No part of this publication may be reproduced, distributed, or transmitted in any form or by any means, including photocopying, recording, or other electronic or mechanical methods, without the prior written permission of the publisher, except in the case of brief quotations embodied in critical reviews and certain other noncommercial uses permitted by copyright law.

ISBN 978-1-7365291-0-2 Paperback

ISBN 978-1-7365291-5-7 Hardback

ISBN 978-1-7365291-2-6 Ebook – EPUB

Library of Congress Control Number: 2022941523

Cover design copyright © 2022 by 100Covers.com

Printed in the United States of America, First Edition, 2022

This book contains an excerpt from the forthcoming book *Gold Diggers: A Sasquatch Attack Survival Story* by Chris Bossy. This excerpt has been set for this edition only and may not reflect the final content of the forthcoming edition.

For permission requests, write to the publisher at the address below.

Pudgy Press LLC

529 N. Franklin St., Fort Bragg, CA. 95437

Email: info@chrisbossy.com

BIGFOOT BROTHERS

I appreciate you!
Thank you so much for purchasing Bigfoot Brothers!
Please do me a huge favor and after you read this
book, take a few seconds to rate it and leave an
honest review on the online store or stores of your
choice that carry my book.
I would love to hear from you!
Email me at: info@chrisbossy.com
If you have encountered bigfoot I would love to
connect with you!
If you enjoy my book please join my email list by
visiting: www.chrisbossy.com
I promise not to bombard you with a thousand
emails but only important updates!
Keep it Squatchy!

To my twin brother Jon.
Thanks for having my back all those times
we've been scared in the dark looking for bigfoot!

1

The B.A.G.

"HELLO, MR. ANDERSON, THIS is a courtesy call from J.D. Caron Credit Union. As you know, the money market account you opened after your mother passed is with us. Our records show that your balance is down to $10,000, and we wanted to tell you the procedures for closing the account since you are down to our minimum allowable balance for this type of account."

Adam's migraine throbbed stabbing sensations into his left eyebrow. He pinched the spot with his thumb and index finger and pulled the skin out like silly putty. It didn't help. He said, "I'm listening." He wasn't really.

Adam had no idea how to do business bookkeeping and it showed. Bills and overdue notices were scattered all over his desk. He had been juggling overdue notices for months on everything. Every week, he had to decide which bill was the closest to going to collections, or which service was about to be shut down. He would negotiate the smallest possible minimum payment to keep things going. Every time his cell phone rang, his blood pressure and stress level rose. And his phone rang a lot. "Thank you, I will see you soon," he said and hung up the phone.

His eyes moistened as he gazed at the family photo of him and his three younger brothers taken at their mother's funeral two years ago. His head throbbed. *Give me a break; nineteen-year-olds aren't supposed to have this kind of pressure.* Adam exhaled, glancing at his poster of Alaska on the wall with the word "DREAM!" written in Sharpie at the bottom and said, "Maybe someday soon." Pushing away from his desk, he stood and went to the railing. Adam leaned over to look down on what was happening below him in the store.

Eric was standing on a box looking up at the fishing line that was suspending the small, orange, two-person display tent from the ceiling. He looked down at the cute blonde who was waiting to buy the discounted tent and smiled his biggest smile and said, "This is pretty high but it wouldn't be any problem for a mountain lion!" Then, wide-eyed, he jumped, letting out a mountain-lion scream and swiped his arm skyward with an opened box blade in his hand. Unfortunately, he had misjudged his distance. The arc of his swinging arm missed the fishing line but caught the nylon fabric on the sidewall of the tent, slicing it from top to bottom as Eric fell earthward. The tent ripped like a sliced orange. Eric landed on the ground with a trip and roll but popped right up, trying to play it off like he meant to do it.

The blonde rolled her eyes at him and then looked at the ripped tent and said, "Never mind," and walked toward the exit.

From his vantage point in the upper loft, Adam was watching the only customer they had all day that wanted to buy something walk out of the store, shaking her head. The pulsing ache in his head seemed to intensify and match the shake of her head. Eric was the clumsiest employee Adam had, and the only non-family employee in his business.

The store was really a ruse to drive people to purchase outdoor adventures that he and his three younger brothers would guide. The hope was that impulsive vacationers would purchase supplies for their trips. Eric was eighteen years old and practically family. He had lived next door to Adam and his brothers his entire life. He was the neighbor kid that nobody thought of as a neighbor because he was always in their house trying to escape the brutality of his dad's addiction.

Adam snarled down at Eric. "Lock the doors, cougar boy; it's time for the meeting!" Adam walked down the stairs and into the back room of the store, his jaw clenched like a vice. He saw Billy, the second-oldest brother at eighteen, but realistically the middle child, being pummeled with pillows from each side by the youngest two brothers, Charlie and Daniel.

They were seventeen-year old twins, and they beat Billy as though they had practiced their timing for years. They synchronized their brains. Billy was covering his face by trying to wrap his arms around his head, which of course left his stomach and ribs open for the next blow. Then when he would respond to the blow by dropping his arms, the next blows would go upstairs to each side of his head with force and precision.

Knowing it would get everyone's attention easier than yelling at them to stop, Adam said, "Billy, stop messing around!"

Billy protested in a voice that was a full octave higher than normal, "The twins always get away with everything!"

The twins shot a quick glance at each other, laughing and saying in unison, "We don't know what you're talking about, Billy!"

Billy mumbled, "Nobody listens to me."

Adam said, "Guys, we are in trouble. We are down to the last $10,000 of Mom's money. We might have to close the store." They all stared at Adam, confused like he had spoken a foreign language. "The ad didn't work," Adam said stoically.

The ad read: *Your adventure is our BAG at the B.A.G. Outdoor Store! Backcountry Adventure Guides are ready to take you on the trip of a lifetime. Backpacking, Rock Climbing, Whitewater Rafting, Fly-fishing, and Horseback Riding all included in one trip, or customize your trip and select 2 of the activities you want to focus on during your trip. All trips are 2-3 days depending on your choices.*

It had been in the local newspaper all spring and summer, and they had put brochures in all the sporting goods stores within a 120-mile radius. Many tourists had called, but only a few had booked an outing. Adam wondered if people didn't trust them because of their young ages.

The small town of Pine Springs had been dying a slow death for the last five years. Every year fewer and fewer people vacationed in their small town. With a population of 1,983, just about every business depended on tourists.

Bed and breakfasts, cabin rentals, three restaurants, the hardware store, two small clothing stores, a donut shop, a candy company, an ice cream shop, an art studio, and the newest venture in town, The B.A.G. Outdoor Store.

The B.A.G. store had a great location between the candy store and the ice cream shop, but the people seemed to spend all their money on the sweets and just browse in the B.A.G. store. They were a month behind on their lease and things looked grim with only a week left before Labor Day Weekend. Labor Day Weekend was always the last rush of the season and then everything in the town would grind to a snail's pace—and commerce, a snail's portion.

Adam's announcement had sucked the oxygen out of the room. He continued, "If we are careful about our expenses, I think we can stay open until December, and then we can have a couple of going-out-of-business sales to get rid of our inventory. Each of us can walk away with $1000 in our pockets and give Eric a Christmas bonus after we close the business for good."

Daniel spoke up despondently, "No! We can't quit now! It's only been one year—all the tourists that saw us this year will buy trips next year. It takes time to build a brand! Next year will be better!"

Looking at Daniel, Charlie exclaimed, "We have to do this. Mom wouldn't want us to quit!"

The Anderson brothers' mom, Megan Anderson, had passed away from brain cancer. It was untreatable and already metastasized when it was discovered. Megan left them the house and $75,000 with the stipulation that they had to spend it together pursuing a dream, rather than dividing up the money.

Billy spoke up, "It's not our fault, guys! People eat more candy and ice cream the first year after a recession ends! They spend extra money indulging on food and treats. We tried to open a store that caters to vacationers right after a recession ended! People won't start spending money on things like this until the third year after a recession ends. We should just close right now and have the clearance sale over Labor Day Weekend. Maybe we could walk away with $2000 each."

Eric spoke up, "What about my Christmas Bonus?"

"Sorry, Eric, it's just business!" Billy said coldly, like he was in the mafia.

In a hurt voice, Eric blurted out, "Oh yeah, Billy; well, here's another thing!" . . . He farted. All the brothers backed away, quickly groaning, "Eric!"

Eric had an intestinal disorder that made his flatulence especially rotten. The brothers had learned over the years that it was best to back as far away as possible or leave the room when Eric released his toxins. At one point or another, each of them had fallen victim to Eric's crop dusting while riding with him in his Jeep, which caused each of them to throw up. With bulging eyes and his hand over his nose and mouth, Adam said, "We need to get out of here!"

They all started running toward the exit when Adam yelled, "No! Stop! What I mean is, we all need to get out of this town and go out into the wilderness to think about this! This life-altering decision shouldn't be made impulsively. We need some time to reflect and think through the pros and cons and ramifications of what we choose. We need to get out of here and find some perspective!" The other brothers stopped en route to the door and looked back at Adam with inquisitive looks.

Adam answered, "We are going to go on our own backpacking trip Labor Day Weekend. I'll get someone else to watch the store, so Eric can go, too! Adam coughed and wiped his eyes with a handkerchief, "For the sake of our customer's olfactory senses, Eric needs to get out into the woods! Everyone agree?"

They all nodded and Eric pumped his fist and yelled, "Yes! Finally, you're taking me camping!"

2

The Trip: Day One

THE WILDERNESS WAS ALWAYS therapeutic for Adam. Getting outside and into the forest felt like he was presenting all his problems to an audience of wise old sages, who lived through many seasons. The patterns on the bark seemed like wrinkles of wisdom. His worries would shrink when he stood amid 150-foot-tall trees. He just knew he would discover answers there.

The brothers met at the store on Saturday with their packs fully loaded. Adam gave his girlfriend, Sky, the keys to the store and told her everything was ten percent off the sticker price until they returned. Sky had called a few of her eccentric friends to help her run the store. He gave Sky a map with their trip plan and estimated time of return.

Adam kept his trip plans secret. He didn't want the twins running ahead, which was certain to happen if they knew the route. Adam planned to leave from the back door of the store and walk right into the mountains. They would hike north for three miles, then follow the ridge east for six miles - then go north again for another three miles and then east another six miles to Gold Digger Falls. Once there, they would make a base camp and explore the surrounding area five miles upstream. On the map, the planned route looked like someone had drawn a picture of two stairs in red ink. Adam planned two days to get to base camp, two days exploring, and one long day for the return trip.

Adam had been wanting to go check out Gold Digger Falls for years, ever since he saw a gold nugget the size of a nickel on an old man's necklace in the town's donut shop. After a brief conversation with the Native American man who introduced himself as "The Chief," Adam learned the Chief found the nugget many years ago when he was just a teen. He said there was a lot of gold just north of Gold Digger Falls, but it was very dangerous territory.

It was rugged country. Too rough for all but the fittest and most experienced backpackers. The maps showed no trails leading to Gold Digger Falls. The area would be pristine and undisturbed. Most backpackers stick to marked trails for safety. But Adam and his brothers were experts, and they had each other's backs. This challenge would be good for them. The unknown factor was Eric. Adam hoped inexperienced Eric could handle this trip.

They made pretty good time and stopped for their first night on the trail in a tree line next to a small meadow. Eric kept up pretty well the whole day, but for everyone's safety, they made Eric hike at the end of the line. Eric sat next to the fire, examining the blisters on his feet. Some people just don't look like they should go into the woods. Eric looked more suited for a spelling bee competition than for an adventure in the backcountry. Eric popped the blister on the ball of his foot and cut the loose skin off. He carefully placed the skin flap into a zip-lock bag and placed it into his backpack. Letting out a sigh of accomplishment, he looked up and saw everybody's eyes looking at him with puzzled looks.

He said, "What?"

Billy's voice squeaked, "What in the heck are you doing?"

"It's a souvenir for my collections," replied Eric.

"You collect blister skin?" Billy said in gross wonder.

"I do now," said Eric.

With a sweeping wave of his hands, Billy said, "Wait a minute! You said collections with an S! What are these collections?" queried Billy.

Eric proudly replied, "I have a jar of my belly button lint. I have a jar of food scraps from flossing my teeth. And now, thanks to you guys, I am beginning a new collection called blister skin!"

Billy said, "You might be the craziest person I've ever met!"

3

Day Two: Gold Digger Falls

ADAM WOKE TO A 5:45 a.m. avian choir practice. It sounded beautiful. One bird would sing a solo. Then, as if competing, another would sing a different melody. Then a cacophony of chirps would erupt from all around. Almost as if the masses were debating over whose solo was better. This went on for fifteen minutes and then it stopped as if everybody had to go to work. Adam smiled to himself and thought okay. He got up and started whistling while he rolled up his mat and sleeping bag. The others stirred, all except Eric snoring away in the meadow.

They all walked out into the meadow. Surrounding Eric, they all turned their backs to him and on the count of three, they yelled, "Rise and Shine!"

Eric looked up and saw a bare butt in front of him; gasping a horrified, "Ahh!" he turned his head away quickly, only to be met by another naked buttock being spanked to add impact. He quickly turned again and boom! Another butt! He shrieked and turned the only remaining direction, hoping to see clear blue sky, but blinded once again by a hairy moon! Eric farted loudly, and the brothers scattered, screaming and coughing as if sprayed by a skunk. Quickly, they hit the trail. Adam hoped they would make it to the falls by 2 p.m., but they arrived at Gold Digger Falls at 4 p.m.

Trail weary, Eric rolled out his bedding and went straight to sleep. Adam and Billy went to take a swim, while Charlie and Daniel went upstream to explore. Charlie had been born first, and it seemed to fit his personality. Always in a hurry to have fun, he was impulsive and always ready to act before his brain had a chance to think things through. If you asked him he would tell you, *"Planning is a boring waste of time that keeps you from experiencing."* In contrast, Daniel was more laid back. He was a follower by nature, which could explain his being born second, six hours later than his twin, finally arriving at 1a.m. the next day.

They hated explaining to everybody why they were twins but had different birthdays. People expect all twins to be identical, but Charlie and Daniel were fraternal twins. They looked like brothers, but there were enough differences in their appearance and personalities that people could easily tell them apart—so much so, that people thought they were joking when they told them they were twins. Then people would ask when their birthday was. Which led to them revealing the different birthdays, and then people would think they were lying or joking. Although they were different, they usually stuck together. Charlie would decide things, and Daniel would follow.

After his swim, Adam left Billy at the waterfall and returned to camp. Adam found his pack opened up and all of its contents strewn all over. On the ground were barefoot footprints. Adam guessed they were size thirteen after a quick comparison to his size eleven hiking boot. Adam looked over at Eric and said, "Really Eric?"

Eric woke up and looked at Adam blurry-eyed, "I've been sleeping! I didn't touch your stuff!"

Adam skeptically looked at Eric's feet and asked, "What size shoe do you wear?"

"Size ten, why?" came a grumpy reply.

Adam growled back, "I don't know how you made these footprints, but you shouldn't have touched my stuff!"

"I didn't do this!" protested Eric. Right as he said this, a golf ball-sized rock hit the ground between them, bouncing twice before rolling to a stop.

They both looked in the direction it came from as Adam yelled, "Charlie, Daniel!" There was no reply. Adam picked up the rock and put the evidence in his pocket. Adam stood there watching for five minutes waiting for them to jump out. Finally, Adam turned and began picking up his stuff. Two hours later, Adam heard Charlie's and Daniel's voices in the distance. They gradually increased in volume, like somebody was slowly turning up the volume on a car stereo.

Adam glared at them as they plopped down next to their packs. "Where have you been?" he asked.

Charlie excitedly shared about all they had discovered exploring upriver. "Steep cliffs flank the river on both sides! The only way to travel upriver is to hike above the river on top of the cliffs. When we find a spot we want to check out, we will have to repel down." Adam, still fuming about his pack, asked, "What size shoes do you two wear?"

"Ten," came the reply in unison.

Adam let out a, "Huh?" and asked, "Who threw the rock then?"

Daniel said, "Not us! It must've been Eric." Eric and Adam made eye contact. Adam looked down quizzically at the rock in his hand.

Late in the night, a tree fell thirty yards from their camp, waking Adam. He shined his light on Billy, Eric, Charlie, and Daniel, only to find them sound asleep. Chills marched up the back of Adam's neck and stood at attention. He moved a little closer to the fire to counter-attack the chills.

He noticed the perfect stillness in the night. No breeze and no animal sounds. An eerie calm filled the air. But then he heard very faint footsteps in the darkness, just beyond the glow of the firelight. Adam strained his ears for ten minutes before his eyes got heavy as a fog of sleep settled across his mind.

4

Day Three: Gold!

SHORTLY AFTER THE BREAK of dawn, they sat around a small fire sipping Billy's cowboy coffee. Daniel opened a pouch from his pack and pulled out a couple of yellow flowers and started eating them. Billy looked at him through groggy eyes as he rubbed his scruffy chin and said, "You know I'm a chef, right? Why are you eating rabbit food when I have perfectly good powdered eggs I'm gonna make for everyone?"

Daniel said, "These taraxacum taste fantastic and they are natural."

"But why would you eat T-Rexum when you can have actual food?" asked Billy.

Daniel corrected him, "No, it is pronounced taraxacum, also known as dandelions! They are entirely edible. You can eat the flower, the stem, the leaves, and even the roots! You can find everything you need to sustain you out here! Eating a mostly plant-based diet really helps your mind stay clearer. When you meditate, you can find the zone so much easier because you don't have brain fog caused by eating a lot of beef. Hindus don't eat beef. I'm not Hindu, but my mind has a lot more clarity without beef."

Billy patted his belly and said, "Well maybe you are okay with being sustained but this belly needs to thrive! And this belly thrives on T-Bone steaks, mashed potatoes and gravy, and corn on the cob. I ain't never seen none of that stuff growing wild out here. I would rather eat these powdered eggs and some beans than your hippie food." The others chuckled.

Daniel looked around, smiling, and realized he had let his passion for plants and meditation erupt out of him again like an active volcano. Daniel grinned and held up two fingers giving the peace sign and said, "I did it again, didn't I?"

Billy said, "Every time!"

Adam talked through the plan for the day to explore upriver and look for gold. "I want us to stick together, no wandering off alone. Yesterday my pack got dumped out and there were strange footprints all around the camp. Then when I was blaming Eric for it, this rock came flying right between us. To top it all off about 2 a.m. last night, something pushed over a tree while you guys were snoring . . . and you will recall, there wasn't any wind last night. Bottom line is, I don't think we are up here alone! There may be a crazy hermit up here or some prospector who wants to scare us away. Let's keep our eyes open!"

Charlie crossed his eyes and said, "Okay, guys, you heard him; keep your eyes open!"

"It's not funny, Charlie. I think we should leave this place," said Billy.

Daniel flashed the peace sign and said, "Don't worry, Billy! This guy is probably just a hippie growing some pot!"

Eric said, "Adam, you're creeping me out! Can I walk in front today?"

"NO!" yelled everyone.

Adam said, "Sorry, Eric, you reap what you sow!"

Eric mumbled to himself, "What does that mean?"

They all fell into line, marching up the trail with their packs. Eric looked behind nervously. He reached into his pack and pulled out a small .22 caliber pistol and slipped it into his pocket as he took his place at the rear of the line.

They hiked up the mountain following the river. It rose higher and higher above the river. Adam led the way, scanning the ground for gold and precious gems. He considered himself an amateur geologist, having taken one class at a junior college when he was sixteen. He went panning for gold almost once a month. His dream was to leave his brothers once they were adulting well and move to Alaska and join a gold-mining company. He was pretty sure their backcountry, adventure-guide-days were ending, and this could be his time to follow his own dream.

They all loved the outdoors. Billy was a skilled horseman and a superb cook. Charlie was in a seemingly never-ending chase for the next adrenaline rush and was a rock climber. Daniel was a great kayaker and guru of whitewater rafting. Adam's expertise was backpacking, fly-fishing, and survival skills. And then there was Eric, an unknown skill set.

Eric was often excluded in social circles because of his eccentricities and gastric condition. He tried really hard to make friends, especially with attractive girls. He had an amazing resilience and confidence for someone who had faced rejection so many times. It probably came from his mom. In grade school, she would drop him off every day at his classroom and whisper in his ear, "You are the best-looking boy in this class!" By the time he was in seventh grade, when most boys are scared spitless to talk to girls, Eric was fearless!

Because of his great self-confidence, all the girls wanted to be his girlfriend, even though he was less than mediocre-looking. The other boys couldn't understand how he did it. Of course, at that age boys don't know how to use their words to ask him how he did it. So, they just beat him up a lot to release their confused hormonal frustration.

Then in the summer before ninth grade, his mom died from a stroke. Grief turned his dad into a raging alcoholic and Eric learned to look after himself. Luckily, he lived next door to the Anderson brothers. It was in ninth grade that Eric contracted his digestive disorder. His confidence stayed the same, but his circle of friends went from hundreds down to the four boys who lived next door. They all spent a lot of time playing outside.

They stopped for a water break about a mile north of the falls, where Adam spotted some interesting boulders and rocks below them at the bend in the river. They planned to rappel down the cliff and spend some time panning for gold. By the time Charlie had secured the ropes and belayed everyone down to the river, they were all starving. They devoured their sandwiches and then got right to work.

They started finding gold. A lot of gold. Adam kept climbing twenty feet up the cliff and digging out a bunch of material. When everyone saw him hold up a gold nugget, the size of a BB, they were all struck with gold fever. They all gang-rushed the area where Adam was collecting material. In five minutes, they had all pulled small nuggets out of their pans. The day flew by, and even though Adam had planned to check farther up the river at least three miles, they had not moved all day.

At about three in the afternoon, they began climbing back to the top of the cliff one at a time. By four o'clock the last person, Eric, was on belay and making his way up the cliff. About halfway up he stopped and yelled, "I have to poop!"

They all laughed and began barraging Eric with comments about dropping brown nuggets, and the danger of mudslides on the cliff. Charlie reminded Eric, "Even though the harness is technically called a diaper, I want it returned to me without any brown streaks on it!"

Eric yelled up with a strain in his voice, "Stop making me laugh! The poop farts are killing me!"

Adam yelled, "I told you to be careful or you would reap what you sow!"

Eric mumbled to himself as he crawled over the top of the cliff, "What does that mean?"

5

The Shooting

ONCE ON TOP, ERIC took off the diaper and ran into the forest yelling, "Bombs away!"

Eric found a big fallen tree to lean against and drop his load. He took his pants off completely and leaned against the tree, letting everything go. While he was finishing up his paperwork, he heard something. A rustling of bushes behind him on the other side of the log. He thought to himself, *That could be a bear! Bears bed or den under fallen trees! I'm about to get attacked by a bear and I don't even have my pants on!* As he grabbed his pants trying to be quiet, his belt buckle clanked and the .22 pistol fell out of the pocket and onto the ground.

The bushes shook violently. He was sure the bear was coming for him. He dove for the gun and came up pointing it at the log, waiting for the attacking bear to crest the log. In a quick flash, he saw brown fur appear and heard a growl. His finger reflexively contracted pulling the trigger even before the idea registered in his brain. The bear screamed, grabbed its shoulder and fell backward into the bushes. It was screaming and rolling around on the ground behind the log.

Eric heard an ear-shattering roar coming from the direction of the brothers. He looked up to see them all running full speed toward him yelling, "Run! Run!" They passed him as he grabbed his pack in one hand and his pants and the gun in the other and took off after them.

The blasting roar that was chasing the brothers seemed to stop when it got to the hurt, screaming creature at the log. Yet the high shrieking screams from the hurt creature only seemed to get louder, the same way a child's hysterics increase when their parent arrives by their side after a fall from their bike. They continued running up the mountain, not sure what was behind them, but sure a confrontation could end badly.

The ridge above the water continued north. They snaked along, keeping the sound of the river's static white noise slushing in their right ears. The wailing shrieks behind them grew more and more distant until the woods seemed peaceful again—except for a heated argument between a stellar jay and a squirrel. The brothers continued in silence. They had stopped running but were still moving at a rapid pace with urgent purpose, trying to create vast distance between them and the nightmare behind them.

An hour later a voice squeaked from the back of the line, "Guys, can we stop for a minute?" All four brothers turned around to see Eric standing there, pantless. Bony mayonnaise, white legs and orange speedo underwear drew all the attention from his lime green shirt. He was still holding his pants in his left hand and the .22 pistol in his right.

Billy blurted out, "Why in the heck do you have a gun?"

"For protection against a bear attack," Eric replied.

Billy flashed, "How did that work out for you?"

"I'm still alive, aren't I?" said Eric.

"Yeah! And now we've got a pissed off mama bear, cuz you probably killed her cub! Don't you know a .22 won't kill a bear? It will just piss it off! Now it's pissed at us! You better hope that cub is just injured and doesn't die right away or that mama bear is going to hunt us!" shouted Billy.

There was an uneasy silence as all the brothers glared at Eric. Eric mumbled as he slipped on his pants, "What I shot was not a bear!" Nobody said a word.

Adam pulled out his map and checked his watch. Then he had the group gather around so they could get their bearings. His best reckoning showed them to be about four miles north of Gold Digger Falls. Since his original plan was to explore five miles upstream of the falls, he suggested they push ahead about one more mile and then make camp for the night. They were all exhausted and hungry, but nobody complained. Somberly, they donned their packs, wanting to put more distance between them and Eric's "Not-a-bear" creatures.

The bush was thick, but they found a game trail that paralleled the ridge just to the side of the ridge's peak. It made things easier except for the slant of the mountainside and the occasional fallen tree across the trail. After a solid hour of hiking the pointy ridge, they came to a small flat meadow.

Adam stopped and said, "Let's make this our base camp." He led the troupe across the meadow toward the northeast corner, which had an enormous granite boulder just inside the tree line. They all dropped their packs with groans and sighs.

"Let's get firewood," said Adam.

"We have forests all around us, do we really need to collect firewood?" asked Billy. "We can just walk ten yards away from camp and pick some up whenever the fire is low."

Charlie chimed in, "Yeah! Besides, we will all fall asleep right after we eat anyway."

To Adam's surprise, Eric said, "If that "not-a-bear" thing comes after us tonight, maybe a fire will keep it from killing us! I don't want to see one again. But I would rather see it in firelight rather than no light!" Daniel stood up and followed Eric into the forest.

Charlie asked Adam, "Don't you think it was a bear?"

"I don't know. I've never heard a bear scream like those things! Have you?" asked Adam.

Charlie turned and ran shouting, "I'm getting a lot of wood!" Adam and Billy turned and walked into the forest together.

6

"Not A Bear!"

IN AN HOUR THEY had a pile of wood the size of a Volkswagen. Billy had a pot of chili beans on the fire and a pot of cowboy coffee brewing. They all sat on their sleeping bags with their backs against the base of the thirty-foot rock face. Adam pulled out his pocketknife and broke a small branch off a log and started whittling. Eric let out a loud burp and said, "Compliments to the chef!"

Billy looked at Eric and said, "You have always been full of hot air, but I appreciate the compliment as long as it comes out of that end of you!"

Charlie asked, "That's all good for now, but where is Eric sleeping?" It was at that moment they realized that Eric had set himself right in the middle of the pack. Adam and Billy were to the left, and Charlie and Daniel were on his right. Charlie, never slow to act, socked Eric hard in the arm. Eric squealed.

Charlie said, "What in the heck was that?"

Eric chuckled and said, "That my friend, was a yart!"

Charlie's eyes got big and his voice cracked as he asked, "What is a yart?"

Eric smiled a mischievous smile and said, "Well when you socked me, it startled me, and I yelped. As you know I have a gastric condition. The jolt of being socked caused a fart to slip out simultaneously as I yelped. So, a yelp plus a fart equals a yart! I yarted!"

Charlie reeled back to sock him again, but Daniel wrapped him up in a bear hug, screaming, "No! He'll kill us all!" Eric just grinned, enjoying his minor victory.

Adam said, "Stop messing around. We need to talk! Eric, I want you to tell us exactly what happened and what you saw."

Eric cleared his throat and began, "I went to poop and I found a big fallen tree to lean against. So, I took my pants completely off and went about my business. As I was finishing up, I heard something moving around behind me on the other side of the log. I thought it was a bear. The bushes were shaking violently and I thought it was going to attack me. When I grabbed for my pants, my gun fell out of the pocket onto the ground. As I reached down to grab it, I heard a growl behind me and I turned around and fired at this reddish-brown furry thing. It was a hairy, person-like thing. It was showing its teeth. I think I hit it in the shoulder."

"How tall was the log?" asked Adam.

"Four feet," replied Eric with his voice trailing off a little. Then talking to himself he said, "It must have been six feet tall!"

Adam said, "So to clarify, this thing was standing on the ground, not the log?"

Shaking his head Eric said, "It wasn't on top of the log, I'm sure of it! I can't get that face out of my head!"

Adam softly said, "What did its face look like?"

Eric continued, "It had dark gray leathery skin, kinda like a gorilla. Its mouth was like ours except wider. Its head was bigger than a human head, but round-shaped. It had facial hair from the bottom lip down. The neck, chest, and shoulders were all covered with thick hair. It kinda looked like it should have hair all over its face too. I guess it looked like someone shaved the hair off its nose, cheeks and upper lip. Its nose was flat and wide like a bad U.F.C. fighter. It looked human though, not like a gorilla or chimp. But what's confusing is the muscles. This thing had shoulders like the Incredible Hulk. They were massive, and it seemed like there wasn't a neck. It seemed like the head just sat connected to the shoulders and chest."

Eric shivered. "When I turned and looked at it, the thing had its top lip flipped back, showing me its teeth as it growled. They were big and square except for the canines which were extremely large like Dracula. It looked like it was yawning at me, except this loud growl was coming from it. And then the eyes—the eyes were the scariest part! Its eyes were wide apart and big. They looked human almost, but bigger and angry. This may sound weird, but the eyes looked dark red. It had a heavy brow, furrowed with hate! It had a look that seemed to say, 'I'm going to kill you!' I think it would have, if I hadn't shot at it.

"When my bullet hit it, it grabbed its shoulder area and started the screaming. It had a hand that had long fat fingers. They were dark gray like the face, but very ashy looking. The fingernails were black and sharp but not like claws. The thing jumped backward clutching its shoulder and that's when I realized you guys were running toward me yelling, 'Run!' You know the rest."

By the time Eric finished his account, he was shaking with visceral fear and his voice was quivering. Billy, Charlie, and Daniel were nervously scanning the dimly lit tree line. Adam threw three more logs on the fire.

"The 'Not-a-bear' was a bigfoot," said Daniel.

Adam nodded agreeing, "Maybe they were watching us?" He took the rock out of his shirt pocket and tossed it into the air and caught it. "We are going to have to take turns keeping watch tonight and manning this fire. We will go in alphabetical order; Me first, then Billy, then Charlie, next Daniel and finally Eric. Each shift will be two hours. If you see or hear anything, you wake everybody up!" They all stared at each other in somber silence.

Eric said, "Oh, yeah! And here's another thing!" A high-pitched fart that started on a lower note and ended on a higher note broke the silence. Everyone yelled, "Eric!" and dove into their sleeping bags to hide their heads under the covers to wait for the gaseous mushroom cloud to dissipate.

Adam's muffled voice came from under his covers, "Eric, someday, you will reap what you sow!"

Eric said, "Why do you keep saying that? I don't even know what that means!"

7

Day Four: The Vote

COFFEE'S AROMA SWIRLED INTO sleeping nostrils, pulling brains from slumber's grip into the conscious world. Billy noticed the stirring in the camp and dug deep into his pack to get a bag of dough. He started patting out some biscuits and arranging them in his pan. He took a stick and spread out the coals of the dwindling fire and pushed some rocks into the center of the coals. He set the pan on the rocks in the center. Adam pulled out his map as he sipped the thick black coffee. Charlie had gone around the giant rock to relieve himself. Eric was standing next to Billy, staring at the cooking biscuits in a zombie-like trance. Daniel was the only one still in his bag at the base of the rock.

Charlie's head peaked over the top of the rock with a goofy grin on his face. He moved over to line up directly above Daniel. He then produced a small pebble and squinted his eyes as he took careful aim at his target and dropped the pebble. It boinked off Daniel's forehead. Daniel's eyes clicked open, almost as if the pebble had hit a switch. Charlie said, "Get up or I'm gonna make a hanger!"

Daniel looked up and said, "You wouldn't!" Charlie hung a droopy slobber string from his mouth and then slurped it back up. Then he did it again, but this time he let the hanger drop. Daniel rolled to the side in the nick of time as the hanger plopped onto the wadded-up sweatshirt he was using for a pillow. Daniel said, "Not cool, dude! Not cool!"

Billy said, "Breakfast is ready!"

Billy and Eric already had their biscuits in their hands. Billy was spreading some strawberry jelly on his biscuit while Eric waited his turn. As they sat around, Adam shared his thoughts. "We are about as far up the river as I told Sky we would explore above Gold Digger Falls. Last night was quiet, so I think we are okay here. My original plan was to start back tomorrow. We haven't checked this part of the river for gold. So, the question is, do we hunt for gold? Or, do we hit the trail for home?"

Billy said, "I vote we go home."

Charlie and Daniel looked at each other, and then Daniel said, "I want to check out the river and Charlie wants gold!"

Adam said, "Well, I want to go home so that's two to two, which leaves the tie-breaking vote up to Eric."

Eric, enjoying the spotlight, started to make a great speech about the pros and cons of each position. Adam cut him off and said, "Never mind, we're staying! Just load up your day-packs. We'll camp here again tonight."

Eric and Billy protested, "Why?"

Adam said, "Perspective. Today I want everyone to think about the store and find out what your heart wants to do. But then, I also want you to think about how that decision will affect each person here. Remember, this is why we came on this trip. We are looking for perspective!"

In twenty minutes, they were hiking east toward the river. It was only half a mile. Once again, they were on a high cliff overlooking the river rushing thirty feet below them. They looked south and saw that the terrain sloped down gradually to meet the river in about two hundred yards.

As they were standing there looking south, they heard a thud and felt a corresponding wave of vibration in the ground under their feet. A loud menacing grunt erupted from the southwest. Their eyes searched for the source like heat-seeking missiles, and they locked on their target.

One hundred yards away, standing next to the base of a big pine, was a black hairy monster. When their eyes met the terror, it flipped its upper lip back showing off its big canines. It reached up and grabbed a branch that was thicker than the business end of a baseball bat. It pulled and twisted, snapping the green branch off the tree with a loud crack pop!

Adam said, "Let's get back to camp!" Charlie, never one to hesitate, took the lead and led them northwest. Adam protested, "Our camp is directly west from here!"

Charlie said, "If we go west we will be walking too close to that beast! We are going to make a wide circle around that thing and over the ridge and then enter our camp from the west side rather than the east side."

Eric yelled, "There is another one!" They looked where Eric was pointing and saw a reddish-brown one standing behind a bush about fifty yards west of them. A smashing knock came from the big black one on their left flank. Then the one behind them let out a blood-curdling scream. The one to their left answered with a reverberating growl so loud and deep that they thought it was ten yards from them, rather than one hundred.

They looked left as they ran and saw the black beast paralleling them through the trees. Charlie shifted his direction to direct north, following the river. The continual screaming behind them seemed to be closing the distance quickly.

Eric glanced back and yelled, "We have to go faster!" They broke into an all-out run.

There were no game trails and they were all jumping through bushes and cutting around trees.

They got more and more spread out. Adam and Charlie were neck and neck in the front. Daniel was trailing ten yards behind them. Although Billy was huffing and wheezing, the husky cook was keeping a steady pace twenty yards behind Daniel. But Eric was in serious trouble. He was skinny and short, which made it hard for him to push through the thick bushes. He was lagging a full thirty yards behind Billy and was losing ground every second.

Eric kept looking behind at the screaming reddish-brown creature who had dropped onto all fours, galloping after him in full charge mode. At large clusters of bushes it would leap right over them like a cat and not even slow down.

Eric started screaming, "Help!" but a drowning roar was coming from the big black one, which was now only forty yards to his left and keeping pace with him easily.

Charlie and Adam burst through the trees into a big clearing with a giant rock in the center. They were about to run past it when an enormous black and silver creature appeared standing on top of it. It hurled a boulder at them, which narrowly missed. Then a dark brown one leaned out and shrieked from behind the rock and showed its teeth. In its arms, it was holding a smaller reddish-brown one that was looking right at Adam and Charlie. Adam and Charlie stopped barely fifteen feet from the pair.

Adam grabbed the back of Charlie's daypack and yanked him towards the rock face thirty yards to their left. He had spotted a small ledge with a cave opening twenty feet up the rock face. Charlie took off and climbed up the rock face like a mountain goat. Adam was right behind him and already eight feet off the ground when Charlie dropped a climbing rope down to him.

That's when Daniel broke into the opening and ran straight towards the rope. By the time Adam crawled over the lip of the ledge. Daniel was right behind him and almost climbing over him. Next Billy burst into the opening and stopped, frozen in fear at the sight of the silverback creature looking down from the top of the rock. Charlie, Adam, and Daniel were yelling at Billy from the top of their lungs.

A boulder the size of a basketball smashed to the ground right in front of Billy, startling him from his shock-induced coma. He heard his brothers frantic voices and ran to the bottom of the rock face.

Knowing that husky Billy wouldn't be able to climb up, Charlie yelled, "Wrap the rope around your chest and hang on!" Adam and Daniel grabbed the rope behind Charlie to help lift Billy. Right as they hoisted Billy over the ledge a baseball-sized boulder hit him in the back of his right leg. He squealed in pain, clutching his leg.

Eric came staggering into the clearing. Only ten feet to his left, the growling black beast walked into the opening and turned toward Eric. Behind Eric, in the tree line, the screaming reddish-brown beast rose on two legs. The dark brown female holding the limp, smaller reddish-brown one in its arms stepped out from behind the big rock. The limp one's head turned, and it shrieked, pointing at Eric.

The massive black and silver one jumped from the rock, landing on the ground right in front of Eric with an earthshaking thud. Eric was now face to stomach with the nine-foot giant. In a fast flick of its arm, Eric's feet were swiped from under him, dropping him to the ground hard. The creatures standing behind and besides Eric jumped forward and stood over him.

From their high perch at the mouth of the cave, the brothers watched as the creatures raised six powerful hairy arms above beastly heads, and then dropped fists repeatedly, pummeling Eric. Only one sound escaped Eric's mouth, a faint wheezing whine. The pounding seemed to last forever.

By the time it stopped, Adam and Charlie were yelling, "Stop!" and "He's dead!" Billy had moved back from the ledge into the cave. Daniel was on his knees with his hands on his head and tears streaming down his cheeks, softly asking, "Why? Why? Why?"

The creatures dragged Eric around to the other side of the rock and out of the eye-line of the cave. The sounds that followed conjured images of a pack of hungry lions feeding on a carcass. When the sounds stopped, the big black and silver one and the reddish-brown one came around the rock and stood there, staring up at the cave. An hour later, they turned and walked off.

In another five minutes, the Andersons looked up and saw an icy stare locked on them, coming from the big black and silver one perched on top of the triangle shaped rock in the middle of the clearing.

8

Inventory

ADAM TURNED HIS ATTENTION to the cave. It was about nine feet deep with a sloping ceiling. It was wide enough for all of them to lay side by side. He found a pile of bones in the back corner. It looked like the skull was from a small fox. He turned to the guys and said, "Let's take inventory."

Everyone emptied their packs onto the floor of the cave. Adam felt like he was being watched. He peered out of the cave to see the big silver and black one's icy stare locked on him. There was no emotion in those eyes, but Adam was certain there was intelligence behind them. Adam said, "We'll call him The Boss." He turned his attention back to the inventory.

They had thirty meters of climbing rope, a climbing harness, a small first aid kit, duct tape, a small stainless steel pot, a Coleman single-burner stove and one bottle of propane fuel, four basic Swiss army knives, one pack of beef jerky, three packages of ramen, four protein bars, two small packages of dried fruit, one Payday candy bar, one roll of toilet paper, four water bottles, four metal cups, two zip-lock bags of cotton balls soaked in Vaseline, four Bic lighters, one biscuit, one bag of mixed cooking spices, four toothbrushes, two dental floss, two small bungee cords, four day packs, two packages of water purification tablets, one bandana, one small notepad and pen, a hundred yards of eight-pound-test fishing line, one bottle of superglue, one package of lifesavers, one emergency survival blanket, one pocket-sized Gideon's Bible, a map, a compass, a small mirror, one headlamp, and one garbage bag.

Adam started reviewing survival priorities. "Okay, shelter: we have a cave. Heat or Fire: we have lighters, cotton balls, the propane stove, one emergency blanket, and a trash bag. Food and Water: we have enough to last us two or three days if we are careful. It may get cold at night, so hypothermia is a concern."

Billy, staring out of the cave at the penetrating stare of the Boss, said, "I wonder if he likes his food frozen?"

Charlie said, "That is probably our biggest survival concern! Will these things leave or will they attack us? I don't think these Swiss army knives are going to help us against these giants!"

Daniel reached in his back pocket and pulled out his harmonica, "Hey! Maybe music will soothe the savage beasts!"

"Your playing will kill us way before it soothes those beasts." Charlie said.

Daniel responded by playing taps.

Adam's thoughts returned to Eric, and he said, "Guys we need to pray like Mom taught us!" Adam started, "Our Father, who art in heaven, hallowed be Thy name, Thy kingdom come, Thy will be done, on earth as it is in heaven, give us this day our daily bread, and forgive us our trespasses as we forgive those who trespass against us, lead us not into temptation, but deliver us from evil, for Thine is the kingdom, and the power, and the glory forever. Amen!" When they finished, they were all wiping their eyes.

"Can we have some water?" asked Billy, holding up his metal cup.

"Okay. We can each have a few swallows of water," Adam said. They each filled their cups with a little water and sat side by side, dangling their feet over the edge.

The Boss, who was every bit of nine feet tall, growled and jumped from his twenty-foot rock perch to the ground. He jumped again, springing another ten yards and then a bigger fifteen-yard jump, followed by one step, and a jump up towards the mouth of the cave. Billy let out a high-pitched scream and threw his water, metal cup and all, right at the contorted face of the attacking beast. The cup bounced off the nose, spraying all the contents sporadically. If they hadn't quickly pulled up their legs, the two clawing fifteen-inch hands would have grabbed one of them. The hands hit the rock face just two feet below the lip of the ledge.

The wet-faced, enraged beast fell to the ground and pounded it with both fists. It bounded on all fours back to the rock forty yards away and ran up the sloped side to the top. A piercing howl erupted into the sky. In the next few minutes, the big black bigfoot, the dark brown bigfoot, the reddish-brown bigfoot, and the lighter brown bigfoot still holding the smaller reddish-brown bigfoot in its arms, all appeared around the base of the Boss's triangle rock. They assembled and turned, facing the cave like a squad of elite soldiers.

9

The Death Threat

THE BROTHERS LOOKED DOWN at the creatures, and the beasts glared back. They stared at each other like two teams of fighters at a weigh-in, sizing each other up. The cornered Anderson brothers were definitely out of their weight class. The smallest bigfoot was the injured reddish-brown one. It seemed to be a young juvenile, but Adam guessed it to be about six feet tall and 200 pounds. Her eight-foot-tall mother was holding her in her arms like she was a light kindergartner.

"We'll call the injured one 'The Kindergartner,' said Adam. We'll call the lighter brown one holding her, 'Big Mama.' She looks like she must weigh 550 pounds. The big black one that flanked us when we were running, we'll call, 'The Shadow.' He looks taller than Big Mama, and more muscular. So, I'm guessing he weighs about 700 pounds. That dark-brown one is short but wider and thicker than the others. Maybe six feet tall, but every bit of 600 pounds! Let's call him, 'Tank.' Then there is that lighter, reddish-brown one, who screamed the whole time she chased us. It looks obvious to me by her pendulous breasts that she is a female. She shrieked or screamed at us like a zombie, so she is, 'The Red Zombie.' I would say she is another seven-footer, but she looks leaner. She might be 350 pounds."

A whoop came from directly below the brothers, to their surprise. A small, black one, about the size of an 80-pound chimpanzee, was facing its family. It had a streak of red hair down the crest of its head and streaking down its back. It was holding Billy's metal cup by the handle. It hoisted the cup up in the air like it was making a toast and it let out a screech! The Boss grunted and the young one side-galloped to the tree line with the cup in its mouth and climbed thirty feet up an enormous tree.

"Let's call that baby, 'The Cup Thief'," said Adam.

Charlie asked, "What's your guess on the weight of the Boss?" Adam said, "He's the biggest. He must be 800 to 1,000 pounds."

The Boss emitted some strange vocalizations that sounded like deep incoherent mumbling mixed with grunting, and it was all strung together, like a long one-word sentence. Tank, Shadow, and the Red Zombie all moved between the cave opening and the triangle rock. The Boss was observing them from his seat atop the triangle rock. He let out a grunt and they started tearing into the ground. All three of them were ripping and throwing turf in a frenzy. The Cup Thief cheered them on by violently shaking the tree top it was observing from. The Cup Thief hooted and banged the cup on the tree, cheering on the frantic digging.

In a few minutes they had a shallow hole dug, that looked to be six feet long and three feet wide and two feet deep. The Boss grunted again, and they stopped digging.

The Red Zombie let out the same liquifying scream it did earlier in the day when she began chasing them. She stood sideways next to the hole and lifted her arms up with knuckles to the sky with long cupping fingers and stretched them in the Anderson brothers direction. Then she shrieked and slapped her massive arms toward the ground and slapped the edge of the hole with the palms of her hands. She repeated this four times.

The meaning wasn't lost in the gap between beast and human. It was crystal clear. Billy said what everybody already knew, "That's a grave, and she reached up and then slapped the grave four times. She just told us that all four of us are going to die!"

10

Billy!

ADAM ANNOUNCED, "I GUESS we better get some perspective on this." It was silent in the cave for twenty minutes. Then Adam broke the thoughtful silence and said, "Okay, it's actually simple—we fight or we die!"

Billy countered, "No, actually, we could die fighting or we could just die."

Adam sighed and said, "No Billy, you are wrong! We are not choosing to die fighting. That isn't a choice! Not fighting is a choice! Which is the same as choosing to die. Therefore, choosing to fight would be the exact opposite!"

"But we could literally die fighting, and by looking at these bigfoots and our situation, I think our only choice is choosing which way we want to die here!" said Billy.

Charlie tried, "Billy, when you get in a fight, you don't plan ahead that you are going to lose the fight!"

"Yeah, Billy," said Daniel, "You do everything you can to win the fight!"

Billy's cheeks were flushing red. He pushed up his glasses and said, "I don't think you understand me! I mean, we could literally die either way!"

Adam raised his voice, "Billy, stop it! You are just complicating the choice. It's simply, fight or die."

Billy started to say, "Literally," but Adam slammed his metal cup against the wall and shouted, "Billy! When the Boss jumped up here trying to get all of us, you threw your cup in its face! You chose to fight! You did not choose to die!"

Billy blinked a few times and said, "Oh . . . I guess you are right! When push comes to shove, I will fight."

"Yes, Billy!" confirmed Adam. "This entire conversation is literal proof that you like to fight! You are wired with the perspective of a fighter. You fight about everything! So, considering that, what is your answer? Will you fight? Or, will you die?" asked Adam.

"I will literally fight!" said Billy confidently.

Charlie and Daniel each said, "Me too!"

"Then it's settled! We have found our perspective. We will fight!" said Adam.

After a few seconds passed, Billy smiled a mischievous smile, pushed up his glasses and said, "But we literally might die."

Everyone yelled, "Billy!"

11
Corn On The Cob

That night, the darkness seemed darker and the hours seemed longer than a normal night. Maybe it was the gnawing hunger slowly consuming their strength. Or maybe it was the thirsty, bitter wind that sucked the warmth from their bodies as though it had punched a straw into a juice box. The only good thing about the night was that they had come up with a plan.

They needed to escape, but the possibility of them climbing out of the cave and slipping away into the woods undetected was impossible. They could not outrun these beasts. They decided these creatures were at least twice as fast as they were. So, they would need a significant head start just to even make it a short distance before being overtaken.

That's when Charlie said, "We are going to have to fly out of here!"

Everyone looked puzzled. Well, everyone except Daniel, who said excitedly, "That could work!"

Billy interrupted, "I literally have no idea what you two are talking about."

Adam said, "Please explain your telepathy, Wonder Twins!"

"The cliff—we jump off the cliff into the river!" explained Charlie.

"Like they did in that old movie, Butch Cassidy and Sundance!" added Daniel excitedly.

Billy said, "Aha! We are choosing to die!"

"No, Billy! You are wrong again! We are choosing to jump! God will decide if we survive the landing!" said Adam.

Billy said, "Or the river will decide."

Adam glared at Billy, shaking his head as he said, "Have faith!"

Billy looked out of the cave, shining his headlamp around, and caught the red-eye shine of a pair of eyes from thirty yards away on top of the rock. He held the light on those eyes for about three minutes and they never blinked a single time.

Pondering out loud, Adam said, "We will need a distraction if we are going to get out of this cave and get a head start—to run toward the cliff."

"The Cup Thief could be our distraction!" suggested Daniel. "If we could get him to run to his tree and climb up it and get all the other ones to follow him, that would give us about a forty-yard cushion and the cliff is about eighty yards away."

"That foot race would be close, but we could possibly make it. How can we get all of them to follow the Cup Thief?" pondered Adam.

Daniel continued, "Remember when the Boss came, screaming and charging when Eric shot the Kindergartner? The Boss didn't run to get us. He ran to get his kid. I figure they all follow his lead. If he runs to his injured kid, everyone else will run to the kid to see what happened."

"So, somehow, we need to injure the Cup Thief and hope he runs up his tree?" clarified Adam.

"Yes! That's our best chance to run to the cliff!" answered Daniel.

Pensively, Adam said, "Now we just need to figure out how to draw in and injure the Cup Thief."

At sunrise, Adam led them in the Lord's prayer again. When they finished, Adam said, "They will be expecting us to arrive back home today. They should start searching for us tomorrow. But it doesn't look good, considering that I left a trip plan that said our base camp would be at Gold Digger Falls, and we made our second base camp about five miles north of there. To complicate things more, five miles north of Gold Digger Falls is the farthest distance I said we would explore. Since the bigfoot chased us at least another mile or two north of there, we are about six to seven miles or more away from Gold Digger Falls! They probably won't get to this area until the second or third day of their search or more if they don't give up. Only a few searchers will be flown this deep into this rugged terrain."

Charlie spouted, "But maybe we could attract a helicopter!"

Adam said, "They won't fly over this area until the second day of the search, and even then, they would never spot us in this cave."

"You are probably right, but we could still hang some kind of flag over the edge of the cave. Maybe they would spot it! Quick Billy, give me your underwear!" said Charlie excitedly.

Billy responded with a hard sock to Charlie's arm and said, "How about I just hang you over the edge of the cave!"

Rubbing his shoulder, Charlie said, "Never mind."

Adam said, "We are out of food, water, and fire! We are in danger of dehydration and hypothermia. If we manage to wait two or three more days, we have three things against us. Number one: They might not find us and call off the search. Number two: We might die before they find us. Number three: If we wait a couple of days to see if they find us and they don't, we might be too weak to attempt our escape plan."

To everyone's surprise, Billy said, "We can't wait! We have to try to escape!" He continued, "My stomach feels like corn on the cob!"

Daniel looked confused. He clapped his hands and rubbed them together like he was quarterback about to have the football hiked to him, but instead of saying, "Hike!" he said, "Explain!"

Billy said, "Well, you know how corn on the cob has all those juicy kernels of corn in nice rows covering the cob?"

"Yeah!" said Daniel.

"Well, picture the inside of my stomach like that, except my cob is empty. But there is a rat running around in there continuing to gnaw on the empty cob! That's what is beginning to kill me! Right now, I am dying a slow, agonizing death. This is a cook's very worst fear! The pain in my stomach is going to get worse every hour. My life is slipping away!" When he finished, he was a little choked up with watery eyes.

Adam, Charlie, and Daniel burst out laughing.

Billy exclaimed, "I'm serious!"

They laughed even harder, and Daniel fell backwards, rolling around. Charlie was wiping tears from his eyes as he laughed uncontrollably.

Even stoic Adam was laughing and pointing at Billy, saying, "A rat's in his stomach gnawing on his empty stomach cob!"

They cackled for two straight minutes and then tried to stop to breathe. But Adam snorted, trying not to laugh, and they all started up again.

This time Billy joined in, pointing at Adam and said, "You snorted!" After three more minutes they were all lying on their backs on the floor of the cave, silently staring at the ceiling.

12

The Bloody Grave

A LOUD CRASHING SOUND on the rock face shattered the still morning silence just outside the cave opening. They all sat up expecting to see the Boss at the entrance again. Their quick look to the entrance was met by a hail of softball sized rocks. They all scooted as far back in the cave as they could while the rocks pelted the wall outside the entrance. Only one rock came inside the cave, blasting the ground right next to Daniel.

Daniel yelled, "Not chill, dudes!" Fearful silence followed the rock assault.

Adam slowly belly crawled to the entrance and peaked out. He said, "Hey guys, check this out!"

They all scooched to the opening. The empty grave was filled with dirt and turf, but there were two bones jutting up out of the ground. A shredded lime green t-shirt was on top of the grave, and it had bloodstains on it. The bigfoots were all standing around it, almost in a semicircle. The wounded Kindergartner was standing next to Big Mama. The Cup Thief was bouncing around, still playing with the metal cup.

The Boss grabbed the metal cup from the Cup Thief and tossed it thirty yards away with a light flick of its wrist. The Cup Thief quickly galloped over to the cup and pounced on it like a cat somersaulting two times with the cup clasped tightly in both hands. It let out a squeal of delight, holding the cup in both hands over its head.

While the bigfoot gathered around the grave, a skinny old bigfoot appeared on the top of the rock. He had long stringy gray hair speckled with red slivers of hair. He had splotchy hair on his body like a bear with mange. His wrinkled face was light gray and spotted with small dark spots. A few random silver hairs on the top of his mostly bald head seemed to cling to their positions like the dazed and wounded survivors left on a scorched battlefield after a great massacre. His back was hunched over.

He stood atop of the rock, looking down like a preacher at a graveside service. Pointing down to the grave he huffed and then pointed up to the four faces peering down at the scene. He let out a mournful, high-pitched, wailing scream. Not far away, a pack of coyotes broke into chorus like they were a choir.

The semi-circle at the gory grave all pointed to the cave and howled. It vibrated right through the brothers' bones like a shock wave. Fear permeated the cave air, freezing every human cell. The old beast jumped down and ran off into the forest. Big Mama, the Kindergartner, and Tank followed the old hunchback.

Charlie started freaking out and screaming, "Oh man, we're all going to die! We're gonna get eaten like Eric! Those bones are stripped clean. They aren't just going to kill us . . . they're going to eat us! They ate Eric!"

Daniel put his hand on Charlie's shoulder and said, "Easy, easy . . . breathe . . . just breathe."

Billy said defiantly with anger in his voice, "No! Cooks don't get eaten! No!"

"At least some of them left! That just leaves the Boss, Shadow, and the Red Zombie to contend with," said Adam.

Billy looked over and said, "You forgot The Cup Thief."

Adam smiled and replied, "Thank God he is still here, or our plan would have fallen apart!"

Just then the Red Zombie grabbed the cup from the Cup Thief and threw it. The cup banged against the base of the rock wall twenty feet below them. The Cup Thief scrambled to retrieve its prized possession, picking it up and clanging it on the rock wall before dashing to his big tree forty yards away.

They had noticed that the Cup Thief spent ninety percent of his time in and around the gigantic tree the day before. They had watched the Red Zombie climb high into the tree with the Cup Thief and lay on some thick boughs and nap for several hours in the afternoon.

The Shadow was usually around the perimeter of the meadow in the tree line. He seemed to move around, changing positions hourly, almost as if he was following some kind of guard duty schedule. Then there was the Boss, who seemed to become a statue on top of the big rock.

He just sat there frozen. The Andersons would forget he was sitting there. About three times the day before, he had let out a loud grunt and changed his position. Every single time it startled the brothers. He seemed to always sit with the sun shining on his silver back, which meant that in the early afternoon he would have his back to them.

"I know how we can get our distraction, but we need to wait until tomorrow afternoon to make a break for it," said Adam.

Billy mumbled, "I'm gonna be pretty hungry by then!"

Adam responded, "We have things to do to get ready that will keep your mind off it."

"You have literally underestimated my mind," said Billy.

Charlie laughed and said, "I just pictured that old cartoon where Daffy Duck and Bugs Bunny are stranded on a deserted island without food and they hallucinate—and they picture each other as a giant piece of fried chicken or a ham."

"Let's get out of here, I don't want to go down that road!" said Billy.

13

The Escape Plan

AT ADAM'S INSTRUCTION, THEY all took pieces of bone from the fox skeleton in the back corner of the cave and began scraping them on the rock wall to make them extremely sharp. They sharpened the longest four bones at both ends. Then they took the smaller bones and also scraped them to sharpen them all to needle-tipped sharpness at both ends.

Adam asked that the smaller bones be about three and a half inches long. The work was tedious. After they had been working about five hours, they had completed the four large bones and seven small bones.

Adam said, "Break time!" They all stopped working and started stretching and rubbing their fingers. They had worked up a heavy sweat from the exertion.

Charlie said, "Man, I am so thirsty!"

Adam looked at him and picked up a metal cup and threw it out into the opening toward the big tree, where the Cup Thief was playing on the lowest branch with his metal cup. Adam threw it fairly hard, but it had only travelled about fifteen yards and bounced twice and then rolled a little.

Thinking Adam was being a jerk, Charlie said, "That's just mean!"

Daniel, coming to the aid of his twin said, "Not chill, man!"

Adam pointed and said, "Look!"

They all crawled to the opening and poked their heads out to where Adam was pointing. They saw the Cup Thief running around bipedal, holding two metal cups above his head, elatedly clanging them together.

Billy said, "Big deal, you made the kid happy. How's that help us?"

"We threw him a cup, and he retrieved it and ran back to his tree, right?" queried Adam.

"Yeah!" said Billy.

Adam continued, "If we throw him a metal cup, he runs to grab it like a greedy little kid, right?"

"Yeah!" chortled Billy, as a smile sneaked across his face.

"What if there are really sharp needle-like points sticking out of the metal cup when he grabs it?"

"He gets hurt!" Billy proudly answered.

"Correct!" Adam continued, like a teacher. "And, everyone, please tell me what happens when a kid gets hurt when they are playing at the park?"

"They run to their mom!" they all answered.

Adam explained, "And sometimes their parents come running to their hurt kid! We are going to make a porcupine cup and throw it as close as we can to that gigantic tree. When the little Cup Thief grabs it, he will scream in pain and all of them will run to him. While they run to him, we will run to the cliff and we will fly to freedom!" They all cheered.

Adam said, "Now I figure we need about ten more of the three and a half inch sharpened bones to make a porcupine cup."

Billy looked at Adam and said with a wry smile, "Man, Adam, I literally underestimated your mind!"

Adam smiled and said, "Touché!"

They all returned to sanding the bones—their spirits filled with hope, which sped their nimbleness and resolve. They had all ten additional bones finished in four hours.

Adam took the third metal cup and duck taped a golf-ball-sized rock inside the cup's bottom to add weight to it. He then waited until the Cup Thief woke up from his afternoon nap and came to the bottom of the tree to play with his two cups. Adam stuck two fingers in his mouth and let out a sharp whistle. The Cup Thief looked up in his direction. Adam threw the weighted cup as far as he could. It landed twenty-five yards in the tree's direction this time. The Cup Thief let out a hoot of delight and dropped both cups from his hands and bounced over to the new cup, and pounced on it, grabbing it with both hands. A loud, angry roar came from the top of the rock. Adam turned to look just in time to see a softball-sized rock flying directly towards his face. He tried to duck, but the rock caught him right in his hairline. He fell backwards into the cave, unconscious and bloodied.

14

The Debate

Daniel grabbed the first aid kit while Charlie and Billy dragged Adam away from the entrance of the cave in case more projectiles were launched. By the time Daniel got the first aid kit opened, Adam was coming to. Blood was streaming down the side of his head, across his temple and into his ear, filling it up like a mosquito's fondue bar.

He tried to sit up saying, "I'm okay!" but he almost passed out again and laid back down saying, "Maybe I better rest."

"Chill dude, I've got this." Daniel said. Daniel cleaned the wound with an antiseptic wipe, dressed the wound with a cotton pad and wrapped Adam's head with a gauze bandage. Then he handed Adam another antiseptic wipe and said, "Here! Your ear is full of blood." Adam grabbed the wipe and scooped out his ear crevices as best he could.

Adam turned over and threw up in Billy's small, stainless steel pot. Charlie said, "You're concussed!"

Billy whined, "When we get out of here you owe me a new pot!"

"Adam, you need to rest and not think too much!" Daniel said.

Irritated, Adam said, "How do you not think? I think I have a headache, but we have to finish getting ready!"

"What's left to do?" Billy asked.

Adam answered, "We need to hammer all those little sharpened bones into the cup to make it weaponized." Adam's eyes fluttered, and he grabbed his head.

Charlie said, "I can hammer them in with this!" and he held up the bloodstained softball sized rock that had hit Adam in the head.

"Ironic!" said Daniel. "We will use their weapon to make our weapon!"

Holding his head, Adam said, "We need to throw it far!"

Thinking Adam's mind was jumbling things up, Daniel said, "Okay, rest! We've got it from here!"

Adam yelled, "No! The cup is too light, and we have to throw it far!"

Billy, tracking with what Adam was saying, said, "We have to add weight to the cup so we can throw it all the way to the tree?"

Adam winced, "Yes, inside the cup."

Billy responded, "Got it! We need to duct tape some rocks inside the bottom of the cup to weight it. We will need to do that first and then hammer in the spikes!"

Adam hissed, "Yes." Then Adam turned to Charlie and whispered, "Cut the rope into four escape lines." He moaned and closed his heavy eyes to sleep.

Billy and Daniel began working on the cup. They duct taped three grape-sized rocks into the bottom of the cup. Next, they began pounding the bony spikes into the cup. Daniel held the cup by the handle and laid it against the rock wall. With his other hand, he held the bone like a nail for Billy to hammer. Billy's hands were too big and his fingers too stubby to hold the bone nails. However, Billy's hand was the perfect size to wield the bloodstained rock hammer.

They pounded away for two hours until they finished the job. Adam, usually a light sleeper, slept deeply through all the racket that echoed in the little cave. Charlie quickly cut the thirty-meter rope into four equal lengths and then started trying to hammer the anchors into a crack in the cave floor. After an hour, he had all four ropes tied off and securely anchored.

"I kind of feel bad that we are going to hurt the Cup Thief," said Daniel.

Billy let out a grunt and raised his voice, "We will die here if we don't! Do you think they will feel bad when they are eating our flesh?"

Daniel yelled back, "I understand all that! I'm not saying we shouldn't! It's just that he's an innocent little kid and it sucks that we have to hurt a kid."

"These aren't people, so that's not a kid." said Billy.

Daniel mumbled, "They seem human-like."

Billy expounded, "At the zoo, they have a sign at the chimpanzee exhibit that says human DNA and chimpanzee DNA share 98.8% of the same DNA. Almost as if the zoo wants you to look at them as though they are human. But they aren't! That 1.2% difference is immense! That equates to about thirty-five million differences between us and them in our cells! We are a different species. Humans have the God-given intelligence to create, because we are made in the creator's image. We create literature, art, music, technology, machines, microscopes, telescopes, airplanes, cars, and the list goes on. These animals definitely have some intelligence, but they aren't human."

Daniel responded, "They were just out here living exactly how they were created to live. They are the top of the food chain out here and we encroached on them! We wounded one of theirs. We are the bad ones here."

Billy looked at Daniel coldly and said, "Eric is dead."

Daniel said, "Yeah, he is, and they are still here . . . waiting for us to die! Doesn't that seem odd to you? They dug a grave and buried Eric. They communicated to us that we will be next. They have us trapped and they know we will die in a short time. Or maybe they are planning on climbing up here to get us. I think they are more humanlike than chimp-like."

Billy argued, "Look, we just made a weapon and their weapon is a rock. We are superior creatures."

Daniel countered, "We spent a lot of time and burned a lot of calories making our weapon. The Boss just picked up a rock and threw it. He hit his target, incapacitating him. Maybe their simple weapons are sufficient for their context. Also, no other animal in the forest can throw rocks, so they are superior."

Billy volleyed back, "Chimps and gorillas throw branches and break trees. Chimps hunt as a pack, with strategies."

"But we've seen them talk to each other and not just a grunt or sound, but some kind of language. Humans have language," said Daniel.

Billy said, "Okay! I will concede that their language differs from the capabilities of great apes—and a bear or mountain lion wouldn't have sought revenge a day after their cub was wounded. But chimpanzees might do that!"

Daniel continued pleading his hypothesis, "What if they are some kind of hairy native people that have always lived deep in the wilderness? What if they really are just giant hairy humans?"

"The fact is, they have committed murder and cannibalism and they are guilty. Justice calls for blood!" replied Billy.

Daniel excitedly said, "Aha! According to what you just said, if they are animals, they are innocent and are just acting by instinct without conscience! But if they are human, they would deserve to die for killing Eric!"

"Wrong!" cried Billy. "If a bear kills a human, authorities hunt it down and kill it! That doesn't make the bear human or innocent."

Charlie had been listening to the debate with interest. He broke in, "These things sure looked tribal to me. That skinny old balding, grayish-red, hunchbacked one seemed to be in charge, like a chief or tribal elder. All the reddish-colored ones left when he left. Well, except for the Red Zombie, who appears to be the Cup Thief's mother.

"The Boss is the biggest and strongest of them all, but he gave up the prominent position on the rock to the old hunchback. That wouldn't have happened in a chimp or gorilla troupe. Maybe the Boss and Shadow are from a black tribe and to keep the peace between the black and red tribe, the Boss took the Red Zombie as its mate . . . or they could all just be one tribe."

Adam stirred from his sleep and sat up. Billy saw Adam move and said, "Adam, settle this. Do you think these things are human or animal?"

Adam looked at him with a confused blink and said, "All I know is they are highly intelligent animals that throw rocks with great accuracy. My head hurts! I don't want to debate right now, Billy!"

Daniel said, "Let me change that bandage, it's soaked through." While Daniel worked on his head, Adam looked across the cave and saw the four anchored ropes. He said, "Bring me the porcupine cup!"

Billy carefully picked up the cup, using his index finger to hold the handle. He brought it to Adam and said, "Hold out your hand, palm up."

Adam extended his palm and Billy gingerly placed the cup's flat bottom onto Adam's opened hand. Adam moved his hand a little, feeling the weight of the porcupine cup. He said with approval, "That's just about right. It feels like a softball. There's just two problems."

"There's nothing wrong with that cup!" said Billy a little indignantly.

Adam looked at him and said, "How are we going to throw it?"

"Oh," said Billy.

Adam asked, "Where's the duct tape?"

"Here!" said Charlie as he tossed it across the cave, hitting Billy in the back. It bounced off Billy's fatty thickness and hit the ground and rolled toward the edge of the opening.

Charlie dived and grabbed the roll just one inch from the precipice. Charlie held it up, showing it like he had caught a fly ball. "Here you go, Adam!"

Daniel finished wrapping Adam's head and said, "I'm going to catch some z's before dark."

It was already dusk. Adam took the duct tape and splayed out four, seven-inch strips, side by side, slightly overlapping with the sticky side up. Then, he laid another four strips of equal size on top of the strips with their sticky side down. The result looked like a square duct tape pot holder. Billy was watching intently, trying to figure out what Adam was making. In another few minutes, Adam had made a second square duct tape pot holder.

He carefully stacked them on top of each other and taped around the top and side edges, leaving the bottom edge unsealed. Next, he slipped his hand into the bottom opening and held his hand up.

"It kinda looks like an oven mitt." Billy said.

"It's going to be a glove," Adam said. He put his hand down and took his Swiss army knife and cut between all of his fingers. Finally, he held up each finger individually and had Billy wrap a strip of duct tape around the finger. A few minutes later, Adam was wearing a duct tape glove that made his hand look fat and swollen. Adam bent his fingers into a fist a few times and then reached down and picked up the porcupine cup.

He squeezed gently at first and then with medium pressure. He felt one spiny needle puncture into his middle finger. He clenched his jaw tighter and set down the cup. He looked across the cave to see Charlie sitting on the opposite wall about two feet from the edge. Adam squinted to focus his eyes better in the last few seconds of daylight. He didn't remember a bowling ball-sized boulder sitting by the front corner of the cave's ledge. Then it moved!

15

The Long Night

ADAM POINTED AND YELLED, "Charlie, watch out!"

The yell startled Charlie, who was dozing off. Charlie jerked awake and saw Adam pointing to his right. As Charlie quickly turned to look, a hairy, red arm flashed through the air reaching for him. Charlie leaned away just in time and a hand hit the cave floor next to him. Still sitting on his butt, Charlie lifted a bent leg up into the air and slammed downward with his heel onto a long finger. He heard a distinct crunch sound, similar to the sound of biting into a piece of celery.

A shrieking scream came from the boulder-shaped head peeking into the cave. Charlie crab walked forward and heel kicked the screaming face. Long hairy arms flailed towards the foot, just milliseconds after the heel hit its mark. The heel kick sent the creature falling backwards through the air with Charlie's shoe in its hand.

A loud thud boomed in the darkness when the beast hit the ground. For three hours straight all the creatures stomped around below, screaming, shrieking, yelling, and occasionally sending a barrage of rocks flying into the cave. Now and then things would stop for a few minutes. Low mumbling chatter would ensue, and then the loud vocal displays and the rock assault would begin again.

Daniel's voice echoed through the dark, "I think they know we are out of fire since we had firelight the last two nights before it was fully dark and now we've been sitting here in the dark for over an hour."

Charlie's voice crackled through the dark air, "It got my shoe!"

"It almost got you!" said Adam.

"We can't chill tonight! They might climb up here and get us!" said Daniel.

Billy anxiously said, "Without lights we can't even keep watch! It's pitch-black tonight!"

"We can't sleep anyway with these things serenading us and throwing us a rock concert. They're pissed! This could go on all night! Where are those long, sharpened bones?" asked Adam.

"Why?" queried Billy.

Adam answered, "Those are stabbing weapons! One for each of us."

Billy said, "Don't worry, Charlie can kung-fu-kick 'em with his other shoe!"

Charlie laughed and said, "The smell of my sock probably killed the Red Zombie!"

"Was that the one you kicked?" asked Daniel.

"Yeah," replied Charlie, "And I think I broke one of her fingers!"

Adam said, "I hope it was the pinky finger!"

Billy queried, "Why?"

Daniel answered, "When your pinky finger is broke, that hand will lose its grip strength."

"How do you know?" asked Billy.

"From seventh grade," answered Daniel.

Charlie remembered, "Oh yeah, Sara the Socker!"

"Explain, please," said Billy.

Daniel said, "During the first half of seventh grade, this girl named Sara would grab my backpack from me. She had this really powerful grip with her right hand. I would pull on my backpack with both hands and she would just stand there holding it with her right hand and laugh. And then, when I was really pulling hard, she would let go and I would fall down. Then she would sock me in the arm or give me a dead leg.

"This particular time, she was chasing me trying to grab my backpack, and I ran into Mr. West's classroom and tried to slam the door before she grabbed my pack. Her hand got slammed in the door and it broke her pinky finger. After it healed, during the second half of seventh grade, she still tried to grab my backpack like before, but she didn't have any grip strength. I could easily pull it out of her hand, even with my left arm! Even after her splint was off and she would sock me, her hand was weak and she couldn't close her fist all the way."

"The crazy thing is Sara kissed him on the last day of school!" said Charlie.

"Yeah! Turns out she liked me the whole year but didn't know how to let me know, so she bullied me," said Daniel.

Laughing, Charlie said, "Good thing for Daniel she moved away that summer or he probably would have ended up as her abused husband! Speaking of strength, how are you doing, Adam?"

"As long as I don't move my head too fast, I'm okay," replied Adam.

"Will you be able to climb down the rope tomorrow and run?" asked Charlie.

"I'll outrun you! You only have one shoe!" replied Adam.

Charlie shot back, "I'm serious!"

"I'm not staying here another day! We are all getting out of here tomorrow!" said Adam.

Just then a barrage of rocks flew into the cave, startling all the brothers. They all faced the entrance with sharpened stab sticks in their hands, ready to fight.

At three in the morning, a thunderstorm came through and the assault stopped. After about twenty minutes, the brothers tried to capture some rain water to hydrate. They hadn't had any water for two-and-a-half days. They emptied their nylon daypacks, which were all waterproof, and opened them wide and hung them outside the mouth of the cave on their stab sticks.

Luckily it was raining cats and dogs and in ten minutes, they each had collected about a quarter of a cup of water. The storm stopped as quickly as it had begun. Now a little wet, the boys huddled together in the back of the cave to stay warm. They stayed awake, staring quietly towards the entrance with their stab sticks in their hands.

16

Last Wishes

AS THE SKY LIGHTENED at the dawning of day, Adam spoke softly, "I was just wondering if anyone wanted to share any last words in case some of us end up in heaven today?"

To nobody's surprise, Daniel cleared his throat as if tuning an instrument before a grand symphonic performance. Daniel quietly said, "If I don't make it outa here, I want my friends to know that I don't want anyone to come out here trying to avenge my death. I just want my friends to stay chill and be their best selves. I even want these things to be chill out here in their element.

"I want people to know that peace of mind that manifests into a less stressful way of relating to people and this beautiful world we get to live in. Finally, I would want everyone to know about how I ate a plant-based diet which helped me be more chill. I would like to thank everyone who chilled with me or let me chill around them."

Billy, chuckling, said, "Would you want flute music at your service, too?"

Daniel, totally missing the sarcasm, said, "Oh yeah, I would! Ask my friend Mandy to play. She's really good!"

Charlie said, "Come on, Billy!" giving him a look. "Do you want that to be the last conversation you had with Daniel?"

"I'm sorry," said Billy. "I'm just scared. When I get scared, I talk trash. I'm sorry Daniel."

Daniel looked at him puzzled for a second and then understanding slowly washed across his face, producing a crooked smile. Daniel asked, "You were calling me a flute-playing hippie, weren't you?"

Billy said, "Yeah, I'm sorry."

Daniel said, "No, it's okay, I like it."

Billy shrugged.

Charlie started, "I love adrenaline rushes as you all know. Stuff like rock climbing, skydiving, snowboarding, extreme stuff. But I want you all to know I would rather spend time together with you guys and grow old than ever jump out of another plane or climb another rock face. There's a feeling I have when we are together that's even more satisfying than all that other stuff, and it doesn't fade away like the endorphins from adrenaline rushes."

Wiping his eyes, Billy asked, "What are you doing to me? There is some strange liquid leaking from my eyes! I am a little scared. This has never happened to me before!"

Daniel laughed and said, "You're talking trash on yourself now!"

Billy smiled. "I like cooking, but maybe you don't know why I enjoy cooking. As you may have noticed, I don't have a way with words and I stink at expressing my feelings . . . but I do have feelings—deep feelings. My feelings come out in my cooking. I can make people feel good when they eat my food.

"I hear people talk to each other and express their feelings when they eat my food. I listen to them. Sometimes I live through them. When I disagree with something they say, I think about it and talk to myself about it in the kitchen. I feel close to people when they eat my food. So, I want people to know that. I want you to know that."

Billy rubbed his hand on his belly for emphasis, "If I don't make it, you gotta have a huge feast with a whole lotta desserts. It's gotta be catered! I don't want no cheap potluck where people show up with dollar-store cookies! And I want everyone to eat first before the service! Dinner and dessert . . . lots of dessert!

"In fact, let everyone have two desserts! Then people can say stuff if they want. Then I want everyone to say the Lord's prayer together out loud. Oh, and when people share, I want them to talk about the best food or meal I made for them and what they thought about or talked about during that meal. I love to cook . . . but I loved cooking for you guys the best." He looked out the entrance of the cave and wiped his eyes.

Adam exhaled loudly then began, "Being the oldest brother sucks sometimes. I always feel like I am responsible for each of you and your success or failure. Even coming on this trip was my plan for all of us. If anything happens to any of you, I'm gonna take it real hard! I just want to say I'm sorry if I have been hard on you since mom died, or if you felt like I didn't let you do things you should've been allowed to do. I was just a seventeen-year-old kid trying to keep us all together and keep you guys safe as best I could.

"I guess I felt like I had to be the man of the house. I want you each to know how proud I am of the man you've become. I think each one of you is a good man. I am proud to be your big brother."

The end of Adam's head bandage came unwound and drooped down in front of his face. Reaching up and tucking it back in place Adam said, "If I can't run very good today, I want each of you to promise me you will not stop running to help me?"

"No way!"

"Not chill!"

"I'll drag you!" came the protesting responses.

Adam put his hands up and shouted over them, "I am responsible for you! The only thing other than

God that I live for, is to see you succeed. That is my calling on this earth! It is who I am! I want you to understand, I care more about you than me! That's who I am! I can't just turn it off today!

"I am the leader of our pack and I say we run! But today, just like always, each of you will go before me! I will run with you, but I will lead from the back of the pack, putting you first just like I have always done! If I am slow, do not come back for me! I don't want to debate it! That is just how it is going to be! Now let's join hands and look at the meadow and say the Lord's prayer."

On this day, the words were especially meaningful. With their hands linked they felt like the four musketeers but they called on a higher transcendent power, not merely the strength of each other. When they finished the prayer, they just stood there continuing to hold hands for another five minutes as they stared across the meadow at their rock-perched adversary, the Boss. Adam, feeling dizzy, but not wanting to let anyone know, sat down and said, "Let's go over the plan."

17
The Athlete

"I'LL SIT OVER HERE and keep watch on these ugly baboon people," said Billy. Daniel grabbed the first aid kit to change Adam's dressing. Charlie lay down near the back of the cave and stretched out, making sure his feet were well out of reach of any long, hairy, invading arms.

Adam started. "When we leave here, we are only carrying weapons."

"I will put first aid stuff in my fanny pack," said Daniel, concerned for Adam.

"Fine," said Adam. "We will just carry our stabbing sticks and leave our day packs and everything else here. If we can, we want to wait until the Boss has his back to us. That usually happens around one in the afternoon. We don't want him to see us throw the porcupine cup.

"We also need the Cup Thief to be playing around the bottom of the big tree. The Red Zombie is usually in the tree line, not too far from him or up the tree in their nest. I think either position for her is fine but I'm praying she will be up in the nest which will give us an extra few seconds.

"The Shadow always stays in the left tree line kind of parallel to the big rock in the afternoon when the Boss turns his back to us. Let's hope he is all muscle and no brains."

Adam looked at his watch, "Our escape window will probably be after one o'clock. We will throw the porcupine cup to the big tree. The second it hits the ground and we see the Cup Thief bounding towards it, we have to be on our ropes climbing down.

"That little Thief is so fast, he will probably be screaming in pain while we are still climbing down the ropes. The very second your feet hit the ground you need to run as fast as you can straight across the meadow past the rock and into the trees until you get to the cliff. Charlie said it is about eighty yards from here. When you get to the edge, you may not have time to stop and look before you jump. Charlie said the water is deep and fast there. If they are about to grab you, just jump as far out as you can without looking.

"Stay in the water and float downstream. Let's get out at the pool after Gold Digger Falls. Today, there should be searchers looking for us there since my trip plan identified that as our base camp."

"Wait a minute! You expect us to go over the falls? That doesn't seem safe!" protested Billy.

Adam responded, "Or you could stay here!"

"No! I'm good, fat floats!" Billy said.

Adam smiled and said, "That's about it, except for one decision. Which one of you is going to throw the porcupine cup?"

"You know I was a quarterback, so I can throw it," Charlie said.

"Yes, I remember you were a second-string quarterback, and you got in one game after that starter got hurt. You completed one twenty-yard pass for a touchdown," responded Adam.

"I threw an unweighted cup about twenty-five yards yesterday, and that was as far as I can throw. It's forty yards to the tree, and we weighted the cup. But it's still lighter than a football and not aerodynamic. It is probably more like a softball!"

Daniel piped up, "I play slow-pitch softball with the church team!"

Adam said, "Yes, I know, but what position do you play?"

"Catcher," answered Daniel.

"Right!" Adam said, "And it's thirty yards from home plate to first base and your throw barely makes it there and a lot of times bounces short. So, we know you can throw a softball about twenty-nine yards and Charlie can throw a heavier football twenty yards, but this thing has to go forty yards!"

Billy voted, "I say Charlie throws it, because the trajectory of a football has a higher arc than a softball infielder's throw."

Ignoring Billy, Adam continued, "I honestly think you would both throw it exactly the same distance. We just need to agree on who is going to throw it."

"What if they only throw it twenty-five yards?" asked Billy.

"The beasts will massacre us before we even get the forty yards to that triangle rock!" replied Adam.

"I got an idea, let's tie this fishing line to the cup handle! That way if the throw is short we can retrieve it quickly and try again!" said Billy.

Adam stared at Billy and said, "You're a genius!"

"Don't tell anybody; I'm just happy being a cook!" said Billy, smiling.

Billy tied the fishing line to the cup handle and unraveled the whole one-hundred-yard spool of fishing line. When he finished, he looked up to see the Shadow walk over to the rock and grunt at the Boss. There was some low guttural mumbling and then the Shadow turned and looked up at Billy and flipped his upper lip back to show his massive canines while he walked over to the tree line to the left of the rock. Billy said, "Guys?" They all looked up at Billy as he said, "The Shadow is in the right position!"

Adam asked, "Where is the Red Zombie and the Cup Thief?" Billy looked over to the area around the base of the big tree and slowly scanned the ground and surrounding tree line. "Not on the ground," he reported as he ran his eyes up the tree, pausing at each branch to check for the red and black bodies. When he spotted them he said, "They are way up in that tree, and they aren't moving, so they must be asleep."

"I bet she's got a concussion!" Charlie said.

Daniel let out a yawn as he turned to Charlie and said, "We were fighting with your girlfriend all night!"

Charlie smiled, "Well, what do you expect, she's a fiery redhead!"

"She might sleep all day!" said Billy and then, "Um, Guys! The Boss just turned his back to us!"

"It's barely seven in the morning!" exclaimed Adam.

Billy said, "I just saw the Cup Thief move!"

Adam yelled, "Get ready!" and he handed Charlie the duct-tape glove.

In thirty seconds, Adam, Daniel, and Billy all had their ropes in their hands and were crouching at the edge of the cave's opening. Adam said, "I will say, 'Throw!' and then when I see the Cup Thief going for the cup, I will say, 'Go!' and we will move!"

Charlie had the duct-tape glove on and the porcupine cup in his hand. Adam watched the black furry spot high in the tree peek down from its nest, positioned with a hairy, red arm cupped around it. It seemed to look right at them.

Adam said, "Hold up the cup and wave it so the Cup Thief sees it!"

A black head moved, tilting to the left and then to the right. Adam said, "Throw!"

Charlie cocked his arm back and sent the cup flying. It arched nice and high as it left his fingertips. It sailed majestically for twenty-five feet and then fell straight down like a dead duck on the first day of hunting season. Charlie looked down and discovered he was standing on the fishing line.

Adam yelled, "Reel it in quick! He's coming down!"

By the time the Cup Thief had made it down to the bottom of the tree, Charlie's hands held the retrieved cup and a snarled bird's nest of fishing line. He shouted frantically, "It's tangled on the glove!" Daniel ran to help him free the fishing line from the glove.

Adam's voice raised in pitch and volume, "Throw it now! He's coming towards us!"

Charlie shook his glove hand in a frustrated frenzy and the fishing line fell from the glove a fraction of a second before the glove fell off his hand and onto the floor.

Adam yelled, "Throw now!"

Charlie bent down and grabbed the glove off a pile of fishing line. Daniel bent down and picked up the porcupine cup bare handed and stood up with arm cocked to throw it. As he squeezed it with his bony fingers, a needle-sharpened spine pierced deep in between his fingernail and skin on his index finger. His hand responded reflexively to the pain and let go of the cup before he could even think about it.

Confused about why the cup hadn't been thrown yet, Adam yelled, "He's twenty-five feet from us! Throw it!"

Billy's fat sausage fingers picked up the cup and launched it like a hardball cracking off a wooden baseball bat toward the left field fence. The fishing line uncoiled perfectly, sailing behind the cup. Seeing the cup fly through the sky over its head, the Cup Thief stopped in mid-gallop and let out a scream of excitement and changed directions, tracking the flying cup like a fly ball. The Shadow heard the little jubilant scream and looked just in time to see the object fly over the head of the Cup Thief, who was following the flying cup like a furry, black guided missile.

The cup sailed past the tree, but the fishing line caught on the big tree's lowest branch, causing the fifty-yard throw to stop short. The cup was hanging suspended in the air fifteen feet above the ground. The Shadow let out a grunt and started hustling towards the tree. The little Cup Thief was bounding full speed towards the tree. They both arrived at the same time.

The Shadow stretched his lengthy arm up to grab the cup, swinging three feet above the reach of his fingertips. He was about to jump and grab it, when a hyper blur of black and red fur screeched, climbing twelve feet up the base of the tree in a split second and leaping out onto the swinging cup.

Adam yelled, "Go!" at exactly the same time a louder brain piercing scream of pain violated the calm mountain air. The Boss was on the move, and so were the Anderson boys.

Adam and Billy were side by side, both running as fast as they could, but looking like clumsy, overweight middle schoolers trying to beat each other to the lunch line on pizza day. Just five yards in front of them, Daniel was pulling away from them like a running back being chased by a defensive lineman. Charlie was a good twelve yards in front of Daniel, running with graceful smoothness and only one shoe.

The Boss had jumped off the rock and was almost instantly at the side of the screaming Cup Thief. The Shadow had grabbed the arms of the Cup Thief and had lifted him straight up but was holding him out away from his body, like an inexperienced Uncle holding a baby nephew with a loaded diaper. The Boss scooped the Cup Thief into his arms and saw a spiked object in the Cup Thief's right hand.

The Cup Thief was shaking his hand with his fingers spread out wide, but the barbed cup was staying attached by two bony spikes that had pierced all the way through the hand, leaving two pointed tips protruding out the back of his hand. With a quick flash of his hand, the Boss grabbed the porcupine cup with his long leathery digits and yanked and threw in one motion, sending the cup bouncing across the ground. Just then a flash of orange color drew the Boss's eyes to the rock.

Adam's orange shoe had passed behind the rock a millisecond too late. A bone chilling growl shook the mountain, and a massive hand pointed toward the rock. The Shadow immediately dropped to all fours and was at full gallop in two lopes. Still holding a screaming baby in one arm, the Boss looked up the tree to see the Red Zombie almost fully descended. He let out a quick chatter and threw the Cup Thief up to an outstretched red arm. The Boss turned and took off running on two legs toward the rock. He slightly dipped one shoulder as he ran by the porcupine cup and picked it up off the ground without even slowing down.

Hearing the heart-stopping growl from the Boss injected the boys into adrenaline overdrive. Billy shouted, "They're coming!" They entered the tree line with only thirty yards ahead of them to the edge of the cliff. The only sound behind them was the dah-dah-dah-dump, dah-dah-dah-dump of a huffing, galloping beast. Charlie reached the cliff first, but stopped and turned around to look behind him. As he turned Daniel flew right past him in a blur, leaping off the cliff. Charlie's eyes got bigger when he saw Billy and Adam running toward him with the

Shadow behind them and gaining ground. He yelled, "Run!" as he reached into his pocket, pulling out a sling with a rock already loaded in the pouch.

Grabbing the cords, he swung the weighted pouch around in looping circles over his head like the blades of a helicopter.

Billy ran past him yelling, "Cooks aren't food!" as he jumped off the cliff and grabbed his knees like he was doing a cannonball off the high dive at the public pool.

Adam was still fifteen yards away and limping badly as he struggled to run with a pain filled grimace on his face. Behind him the Shadow rose from his four-limbed gallop up onto two legs. He was just five yards behind Adam and closing.

Charlie yelled, "Adam duck!" and let go of all the cords, sending the rock filled pouch flying with all the cords trailing behind. Adam ducked at the same time a hairy arm extended grasping for his head. It only found air.

It was the same air that the flying projectile was whistling through like a bullet. The rock squished right into the Shadow's eyeball at the same time the creature tripped over Adam who was crouching on the ground in the fetal position, covering the back of his neck with his fingers interlaced as though expecting a neck snapping bite. While the Shadow rolled on the ground clutching his face, Adam scrambled to his feet and ran towards Charlie.

As they jumped off the cliff, a bony metal cup hit Charlie in the back digging deep into his flesh.

Bursting up out of the water to gasp for air, Adam looked up at the edge of the cliff to see the hulking Boss screaming. His beastly yell gradually faded from the boy's ears as the rushing torrent swept them rapidly downstream. Adam thought to himself, *Just because I can't hear him anymore, doesn't mean he isn't still screaming about our escape.* This thought seemed to warm him as he looked downstream and spotted each of his brothers floating on their backs with their feet up in front of them. He yelled and waved. They all looked back, giving him the thumbs-up sign.

18

The Doctor

ADAM KEPT GLANCING UP to the tree-lined cliffs on his right. He kept expecting to see hairy silhouettes running through the trees or basketball-sized boulders being thrown down onto their heads. A shower of relief washed over him when he heard the thwop-thwop-thwop-thwop sound of the helicopter flying over them. The chopper buzzed ahead of them down the river and in twenty more minutes they were being fished out of the river by the sheriff's search and rescue team just above Gold Digger Falls. Well, all of them except Billy, who missed the safety rope and took the ride over the falls, screaming hysterically.

After the chopper landed in the clearing below the falls, they gave the boys water and some dry sweats, wool socks and beanies to change into. Each of them received a bag of trail mix and another bottle of water before the chopper lifted off. As they lifted into the blue sky, they all shouted with big grins on their faces.

The doctor that checked them out at the hospital noticed they all had minor scrapes and cuts of no real consequence, except for Charlie. Four deep punctures in the center of Charlie's back intrigued the doctor. They were very close to his spine. The doctor asked Charlie how it happened.

Charlie said, "I don't know!"

The adrenaline rushing through his body as he jumped off the cliff followed by the cold rushing water of the river masked any pain he would have normally felt from such punctures.

They gave Adam a C.T. scan and cleaned and re-bandaged the wound on his head. The doctor said it was too late for stitches and that he would have a nice scar. The doctor diagnosed Adam with a concussion and asked him how it happened. Adam told him he had hit his head on a rock. They had all been examined and were ready to go home. Adam's girlfriend had arrived and was ready to take them home. The doctor came back into the room and asked them all to strip again.

The nurse began to unbandage Adam's head.

Billy exclaimed, "They have already examined me! We want to go home now! What's going on here?"

The doctor and the nurse looked at each other, and the doctor said, "We forgot to take photos of all of your bodies to document your injuries."

"I'm not injured!" said Billy.

"On the contrary, you have minor cuts and scrapes all over your hands and arms and some puncture wounds in the palm of your bandaged right hand," said the doctor in an authoritative tone.

"Minor cuts and scrapes are literally not an injury! If they were, this place would be packed all the time with kids needing you to put bandaids on their scraped knees and elbows. What kind of insurance fraud are you trying to pull here?" asked Billy incredulously.

"We will not charge you, sir, for the treatment of your scrapes and minor cuts," offered the nurse.

Defensively, the doctor said, "I am going to prescribe you something for the punctures on your hand."

Billy shook his head as he spoke, "I will not be picking up that prescription! I have Neosporin at home and I can literally treat my 'injury' at home, so why do you think you need photos of my body?" asked Billy beginning to escalate his voice in anger.

Adam, Charlie, and Daniel had stripped down to their underwear and were all watching Billy do his thing. Maybe it was because he was husky, or maybe it was a strong conviction about personal privacy. Nobody really knew why, but Billy had been like this about his body since middle school. He had thrown such a fit that the P.E. teacher finally started letting him change his clothes every day in the custodian's supply closet.

In high school, Billy went to the bathroom and changed in a locked stall every day. If the doctor and the nurse weren't there, he probably wouldn't have had any problem getting naked in front of his brothers. But the doctor had already examined his body once, and now he wanted to take another look and take pictures?

"No!" Billy yelled.

The doctor looked at the other brothers and said, "Can you help me out here?"

Adam said, "I think he's right" and reached for his sweatpants. Seeing Adam's move, Charlie and Daniel redressed. The doctor shook his head and stormed out of the room.

The second the door swung shut behind the doctor, the nurse whispered, "There is a detective and the district attorney outside and they have been asking us about your injuries and they asked the doctor to take pictures for them. They said something about a guy named Eric who is missing."

She quickly re-bandaged Adam's head while she was talking.

Billy said, "Let's go!"

Adam looked at the nurse and asked, "Can we go?"

The nurse replied, "The doctor already signed off on all your discharge papers and was on his way to tell you when the detective stopped him and handed him the camera. The doctor said something about weird puncture wounds and the concussion and said he thought you were all in a fight."

Billy got up and raised his voice to a shout, "We are leaving now!" and walked out of the room. The others followed.

The nurse slipped out a mousy, "Sorry," as the door swung shut behind them.

They walked past the doctor standing with the detective and the district attorney.

Adam said, "We'll come to the police station and talk to you at 3 p.m. tomorrow. We are exhausted, and we are going home now." Adam slipped his hand around Sky's shoulders to steady himself as they walked out.

The district attorney snarled after them, "We are taking pictures tomorrow!"

19
Randy's Burgers

THEY STOPPED AT RANDY'S Burgers, a small, hole-in-the-wall hamburger joint. They each ordered two greasy hamburgers, two steak fries, and a chocolate malt. Randy's served chocolate malts in a silver metal cup with an empty glass mug. There was always enough malt in the tall silver cup to fill up the glass mug one and two-thirds times. So, it was really like getting two malts for the price of one. Randy's was the place they came every week after church.

As they inhaled their food, Sky placed her hand on Adam's arm and asked, "What happened to Eric?" They all stopped chewing at the mention of Eric's name.

With a glazed look in his eyes and a low voice, Adam said, "Bigfoot is real, and bigfoot killed Eric."

Sky's jaw dropped open as she looked around at the brothers. Daniel turned his head and wiped a tear.

"Guys, when you talk to the cops and the district attorney tomorrow, they will not buy this story!" said Sky.

Billy raised his voice and said, "It literally happened! It's not a story!"

"I believe you but this stor . . . um, I mean your account of events is unbelievable!" said Sky.

"We will just tell them everything that happened and hope they believe us," replied Adam.

"Yeah!" said Charlie. "We aren't going to make something up so they will believe us. We are not liars! We will just tell them the truth and they have to believe us. We experienced this! It happened to us! They may not believe in bigfoot, but we know they're real! Maybe they will believe that we believe what we are saying even if they don't believe in bigfoot!"

"They might think we believe our story, but then again they might think we are all mental and put us in padded rooms!" added Daniel.

"Guys, we can't worry about what they think! We all just need to go home and shower and get some sleep!" said Adam as he rose to his feet. They got up and cleared their trash and filed out the door towards Sky's truck.

As the truck drove off, a man who had been sitting at a corner table of Randy's little joint adjusted his baseball cap and went to the counter to talk to Randy about what he had just heard. After a five-minute conversation, the man stepped outside and dialed a number on his cell phone.

"Hi boss, send me a camera crew! I've got a story for tomorrow's news that's gonna go national! Give me an hour and I'll email you the outline of what's happening here. Just trust me, it's going to be big! . . . It's about a murder!" The reporter turned and stepped back into Randy's, ordering a diet coke and an order of fries to go.

20

The Great Dane

THE CHIEF DETECTIVE WAS shocked when he looked out the window of the police station at noon and saw a television news crew filming. He was even more shocked to turn away from the window and see the same news reporter from outside, speaking on the television across the room on the wall.

He yelled, "Turn that up!" Everyone stopped what they were doing and gathered around. The reporter from Randy's was in front of the camera.

"Seven days ago, four brothers and an acquaintance of theirs, named Eric Grimes, went into the woods. After they missed their return date by two days, the Pine Springs Search and Rescue Team began a full search. They found the Anderson brothers, but Eric was not with them. It seems the district attorney and police detectives suspect foul play after discussing the boys' wounds with the emergency room doctor. This afternoon the

Anderson brothers are coming to the Pine Springs police station to tell their story.

"Last night I heard them say firsthand that bigfoot killed their friend, Eric. That's right! Even though it sounds crazy, all four brothers claim bigfoot murdered Eric! But what is the explanation for their injuries? These Bigfoot Brothers own and operate a backcountry adventure guide service. Why would they have trouble in the woods? Why would they all have injuries that look suspicious to authorities? Maybe bigfoot will come out of these mountains and confess.

"In the meantime, the Bigfoot Brothers have a lot of questions to answer. One thing is for sure, I will keep my eye on this story as it unfolds. This is Robert Hawk, reporting live from the town of Pine Springs, the home of the Bigfoot Brothers."

When the Anderson brothers finally walked into the station twenty-eight minutes late at 3:28 p.m., the district attorney and the chief homicide detective were livid. It took a good twenty minutes for Adam, Charlie, and Daniel to convince Billy to come with them. Billy was not excited about them taking photos of his body. He felt their attempt last night to get photos deceptively through the doctor revealed that the authorities had already decided their guilt and would lie and violate their rights to get their desired outcome. Billy tried to convince the brothers to hire a lawyer. They finally convinced Billy that they had to go in and tell them what happened, or the authorities would think they were guilty for sure. Reluctantly, Billy gave in.

When they walked into the station, the chief of detectives sneered sarcastically as he commanded, "Show the 'Bigfoot Brothers' to their changing rooms!"

As Billy passed by, the chief sarcastically said, "Take a lot of pictures of this one!"

Billy replied, "Why? Are you a perv?" Officers in the room turned their heads away quickly to hide their snickers.

"We are called the Anderson brothers!" corrected Adam.

The district attorney huffed, "According to your friend, Robert Hawk from the news, you are the 'Bigfoot Brothers' and you are saying bigfoot murdered Eric!"

Adam started to respond but the district attorney put his hand up and said, "We'll listen to your fairy tale after we get pictures."

"We literally want our attorney present first!" said Billy, red-faced.

The other brothers all said, "Yes! Yes, we do!"

"Billy's right!" confirmed Adam.

Adam called the only attorney he knew. A skinny, balding, bespeckled man named Godwin Dane, professionally known as G. Dane, Attorney at Law.

G. Dane was the same attorney who helped Adam when he was seventeen years old to fight to keep custody of his brothers after their mom died. When Godwin received Adam's phone call, he was only two miles from the station. He had seen the news and left his house after packing a suitcase and telling his wife he had to go help the Anderson boys.

She yelled, "You're retired!" as he pulled out of the driveway.

After G. Dane arrived at the station, he met with the boys privately and listened to them tell him their story for about two hours, stopping them occasionally to ask questions and scribble on his legal pad.

When he emerged from the room, he told the waiting chief of detectives and district attorney, "No pictures of their bodies without a warrant! They are cooperating with your investigation. Get a helicopter and a forensic body recovery team. The boys will take you to Eric's body and tell you what happened to him at the site. Call me when you have the chopper and we will all go."

As they walked out of the station with G. Dane leading the procession, Billy turned around and yelled to the chief of detectives, "No pictures today!"

As they exited the building, Adam said, "I know your name is Godwin Dane, but from now on we are calling you the Great Dane! No more of this G. Dane nonsense!"

G. Dane looked at them all and smiled. He didn't have the heart to tell them about the merciless teasing he endured throughout his childhood school days. The other kids called him, "The Gimpy Dane" because of his last name and small stature. Even though he was old now, he enjoyed being recognized as great rather than inadequate.

He smiled and said, "Thanks, guys! I think things are going to be just fine!"

Before the boys realized what was happening, a man was standing in front of their car speaking into a microphone.

"The Bigfoot Brothers have just walked out of the police station! Hello, guys, does this mean you are innocent?"

The Great Dane put his hand up stepping in front of the camera saying, "I'm attorney G. Dane and I can let you know now, these boys are completely innocent and will be taking the authorities to Eric's body in the next few days."

Robert Hawk responded with, "So is it true that bigfoot murdered Eric?"

The Great Dane said, "We have no further comments at this time!" He motioned for the boys to get in the car and leave.

The reporter turned to his cameraman and said, "Cut! Let's see if we can talk to the D.A. or a homicide detective!" They turned and walked toward the police station as the Anderson brothers drove away.

21
No Pictures!

ALL THE MAJOR NEWS outlets broadcast the story that evening. The next day news vans started rolling into town and setting up in front of the police station and the courthouse. Reporter Robert Hawk scooped them all again by interviewing Adam's girlfriend, Sky, while she was running the B.A.G. Store for Adam. He started off by asking about the business and about each brother's role in the business.

Next Robert Hawk asked about Eric and how long he had known the brothers. He asked her to describe his personality. Then, searching for a motive, he asked about the struggling business and the need for publicity, suggesting that this was possibly just a big publicity stunt. Sky replied with the fact that the boys were all extremely dehydrated when they were found. Robert used that opening to ask about the boys' physical injuries.

"Is Eric still alive out in these mountains? If so, how long do you think he will live?"

Sky looked down and said, "He would be dead by now."

Hawk followed up with, "If they left him out there, wouldn't that be the same as murder?"

She looked up with a glare, realizing his carefully crafted interview had led her to this, his number one question. She said, "Some animal out there killed Eric. I don't believe in bigfoot, but I believe in these brothers. If these brothers say bigfoot murdered Eric, then some hairy animal murdered Eric! Maybe it was a bear. I guess the authorities can figure out what animal killed Eric after the boys take them to the body!"

"They're going to the body?" asked Hawk.

"I'm done talking!" said Sky.

Robert Hawk and his cameraman finished the rest of the piece outside in front of the store.

His closing hook was, "The Bigfoot Brothers mystery continues to raise more intriguing questions about the disappearance of Eric Grimes. Is it a publicity stunt? Was there an animal attack in the woods? Have these brothers concocted a story to hide what they have done? How did these four experienced wilderness guides end up with their injuries? Was there a fight? Was it premeditated murder? Was it bigfoot as the Bigfoot Brothers are claiming?

"The Bigfoot Brothers know where Eric's body is, and if we are to believe them, so does bigfoot!

When they take the authorities to the body, will the authorities see bigfoot too? This is Robert Hawk reporting to you from Pine Springs outside the Bigfoot Brothers' store. I will keep my eye on this drama as it unfolds, giving you the Hawkeye view, and I will see you on channel KRST. Remember, you heard it first on KRST!"

The interview broadcast nationally on the evening news. By the next day, more news trucks and salivating reporters invaded Pine Springs like a ravenous army of ants. Tourists also began flooding the town. All the hotels were full and Randy's Burgers and all the food places had lines of people out the doors. But the absolute longest line of people was outside the B.A.G. Store.

Reporters, tourists, and amateur bigfoot hunters were all coming to the store looking for Bigfoot Brothers' merchandise and maps of the local mountains.

Every customer wanted to ask Sky questions about the Bigfoot Brothers. After the first hour of trying to say, "No" diplomatically in a hundred different ways, Sky yelled to the crowd, "I AM NOT answering any more questions about the Bigfoot Brothers, period! And NOBODY has permission to take my picture UNLESS YOU BUY SOMETHING!"

To her great surprise only a few people left. In two more hours, every item in the store under twenty dollars was sold, and then she had people asking her if they could just pay her for a photograph with her.

When Adam and the brothers pulled up to the store, people and reporters mobbed their vehicle. Daniel got out of the car first, giving the peace sign saying, "Chill!" Next, Charlie got out of the car and started giving people high fives as he cheesed and flexed for pictures.

Billy anxiously yelled, "I'm staying in the car!" as he rolled up his window and locked the door.

"I wish I could too!" mumbled Adam as he exited the driver's side of the vehicle and cut his way through the crowd and into the store. He spotted Sky across the store in the corner posing for a photo with a family. Two news cameras were filming Charlie and Daniel near the cash register signing autographs.

A reporter across the room had seen Adam walk through the front door. He started dodging left and right through the crowd, moving quickly towards Adam, like a predator stalking its prey. Adam moved left circling the counter and grabbed Charlie and Daniel by the collars, pulling them towards the back room.

He yelled, "Sky! Meeting, now!" He pushed through the swinging doors into the warehouse. A minute later, Sky came bouncing into the room with a big smile, holding a shoebox under one arm and a business card in her hand.

Adam shouted, "Don't pose for pictures! Don't sign autographs! And definitely don't give news interviews!" His voice raised slightly and his eyes gave a strained look at Sky.

She answered, "I know I messed up bad, but look!" And she opened up the shoe box to reveal a sea of twenty-dollar bills. Beaming, she said, "And there's about ten thousand dollars in the cash register!"

"Dude!" exclaimed Daniel.

"How?" asked Adam.

Sky explained the morning events and exclaimed, "Everyone is asking for Bigfoot Brothers merchandise!"

Charlie responded, "Let's give the people what they want! Let's order some T-shirts, hats, jackets, backpacks, and coffee mugs with Bigfoot Brothers on them!"

"This might all stop tomorrow and then we will be stuck with unsellable merchandise!" reasoned Adam.

"I've never seen so many people in this store! I would rather give the store another shot rather than close down or do a closeout sale," countered Daniel.

All eyes looked to Adam for a decision. Adam sighed and said, "Okay, but just T-shirts and hats! They will say, "Bigfoot Brothers" on them. I want them to be all black. The font can be white. Let's do both, long-sleeved and short-sleeved T-shirts and adult and children's sizes."

Turning to Sky he asked, "What sold out first today?"

"Maps of these mountains and water bottles!" answered Sky. "Okay, we'll restock the maps and get water bottles printed up, too."

"Same design as the shirts? Black bottles with white letters that say, Bigfoot Brothers on them?" asked Sky.

"Yes!" said Adam.

"Use all the money we made today and put a rush order on everything! Oh yeah! One more thing . . . order a vinyl banner that says, 'Bigfoot Brothers!' to hang over the wooden sign on the roof. Under 'Bigfoot Brothers' have it say, 'Outdoor Store' in smaller writing!"

"Why not adventure guides?" asked Charlie.

"I'm not sure I can hike in the woods anymore now that I've seen bigfoot," answered Adam.

Thinking about Adam's words, Charlie and Daniel gave each other a look of agreement. Adam looked over at Sky to see her looking at a business card in her hand like it was a winning lottery ticket.

"What is that?" he asked.

She smiled and said, "One of the men that took my picture out there is a modeling agent! He said I could be a model for women's clothing and activewear for outdoor and hunting and fishing stores! He said I have a week to decide, or he would find someone else."

Before Adam could respond, Billy came busting in the door with a jacket over his head, yelling, "No Pictures! No pictures!"

Uncovering his head, he said, "Guys, the Great Dane called! We gotta be at the sheriff's station in twenty minutes to take them to Eric! The Great Dane is coming with us!"

"I'm taking one of these! Said Daniel as he grabbed a Bowie knife off a shelf."

"I'm taking two!" said Billy as he grabbed them like he was at a black Friday sale.

"We are going with the cops, guys! They will be armed!" said Adam.

Charlie picked up a Bowie knife for himself as he said, "Remember, Eric had a gun, too!"

"Let's go!" said Adam as he grabbed a can of bear spray as he walked toward the door.

"I'll order everything today!" said Sky cheerfully.

Billy put his jacket over his head and ran out into the store yelling his "No pictures!" mantra again.

Sky clicked a few buttons on the computer keyboard and then looked up at the clock. Next, her eyes locked like a magnet back onto the shiny business card in her hand. She smiled to herself and walked back into the store with the shoebox of cash under her arm announcing, "Pictures with Bigfoot Brother Adam's girlfriend, twenty dollars!"

22

The Investigation

AN HOUR LATER, TWO helicopters landed in the tree-lined meadow with a tall, triangle-shaped rock in the center. The detective tried to confiscate the boys' hunting knives but the Great Dane stopped him, explaining that they were hunting knives and that they were in a national forest where large knives and even loaded guns were legal for citizens to walk around with.

The detective's eyes bulged like the arteries in them were bursting. He asked excitedly, "Do they have loaded guns on them?"

The Great Dane peered at him with a straight face and said, "No, but I do! So, let's do what we came here to do before we all get attacked by bigfoot!"

The detective scoffed and said, "Okay boys, where did you put the body?"

Having landed on the river side of the triangle rock, Adam, Billy, Charlie, and Daniel had all huddled side by side with their knives gripped by tight-fisted, white-knuckle grips. Adam's hand trembled with the can of bear spray. Their heads were on swivels and their eyes kept going up to the top of the rock. In their adrenaline-laced fear, they hadn't even heard the exchange between the Great Dane and detective Stewart. The district attorney had been standing back and observing the boys.

He noticed them looking up repeatedly at the rock and got a picture in his mind of Eric on the top of that rock with a sharpened stick and a baseball sized rock. He could vividly see these four brothers surrounding the rock. He imagined the brothers reaching up to get him and getting stabbed in the hands. He imagined a rock being hurled down at Adam, the obvious leader of the brothers. He pictured the rock striking him in the head and knocking him unconscious.

He envisioned the other brothers all running to their fallen brother, while Eric jumped down. Having incapacitated the leader, he saw Eric run up and attack Charlie, the most fit brother, by stabbing him multiple times in the back with his sharp stick.

He could picture Daniel yelling, "Stop it! Stop it!"

He imagined Billy responding by picking up the rock that had hit Adam in the head and caving in Eric's skull by striking it an excessive number of times because Billy obviously has severe anger issues. He imagined all of this in a few seconds with his sharp legal mind. Now all he needed was Eric's body.

The Great Dane walked up beside Adam and whispered, "Where is Eric?"

Adam stepped forward and the brothers walked with him almost as if they were in a marching band formation. They circled the rock and stopped at the shallow grave with a bone sticking out of the ground. The tattered bloody shirt that was previously attached to the bone like a grotesque flag of death was gone. Adam pointed down, and the brothers backed away, looking up nervously to the cave and over to the big tree.

"Can we wait in the chopper?" asked Daniel.

"No!" said Detective Stewart, "This is a homicide investigation and while we are here, you are going to tell us what happened!"

Adam started to speak, but the Great Dane grabbed his arm and he stopped mid-sentence.

The Great Dane suggested, "How about you wait until you get the forensic results on this body and then maybe these boys will tell you what happened here?"

"Nice try," the detective said. "We are at the scene of the crime with parties who were involved in the crime or at least witnesses to the crime. They have not been charged with anything yet, but if they will not share what they know about Eric's death, I will arrest them all for impeding a police investigation."

The district attorney chimed in, "I promise you, Mr. Dane, that if they do not cooperate today, I will prosecute them for obstruction of justice, and make sure they pay for the cost of hiring these choppers and all the man hours that this is costing the taxpayers today! Probably about sixty thousand dollars!"

"Fine!" capitulated the Great Dane. "They will tell what happened here, but your very presence here, Mr. District Attorney, will almost guarantee these boys a mistrial should you bring any action against them. Your presence here as the chief prosecutor shows that you are using your power to influence these detectives to prove the outcome you desire, rather than letting them investigate without bias as they normally would without your presence. Your very presence here is enticing them to please you and earn accolades from you!"

A vein in the District Attorney's forehead bulged as his face reddened. He turned to Detective Stewart and said, "Record everything, and take good notes and pictures!" He turned and walked to the chopper. The Great Dane patted Adam on the shoulder and he began.

As Adam shared the series of events, Charlie, Daniel, and Billy kept interjecting left out details. Adam was just trying to give the skeleton of their account and not include all the tendons and muscles, because this is what the Great Dane had previously discussed with Adam. After their third interruption, the Great Dane signaled for the boys to be silent, by holding a finger to his lips when detective Stewart was looking down and writing on his notepad.

Detective Stewart didn't lift his eyes or his pen, but wrote in parentheses in his little book that Adam wasn't sharing every detail on purpose. His peripheral awareness of his surroundings and reading the body language of people he interviewed often revealed as much as their words. He made an asterisk in the margin and looked up.

When Adam finished, Detective Stewart called over the photographer and asked him to take pictures and video of the cave, the tree line, the triangle rock and, of course, the grave and its contents. He asked another technician to measure from the triangle rock to the base of the cave's rock face. The medical examiner came up and pulled the detective aside. The detective looked up, smiling and laughing. The detective came back to Adam and asked him to take him to where they jumped into the river. He asked for the photographer to come with them.

Once at the spot, the detective looked down and smiled to himself. The detective turned to the Great Dane and the boys and said, "Okay, we're done here!"

The photographer snapped a few photos and some video of the river below and walked back toward the chopper, while detective Stewart counted his paces from the cliff's edge back to triangle rock. When he was twenty paces from the cliff he snagged something with the toe of his shoe. He looked down and saw a nylon pouch with three pieces of climbing rope tied to it. He looked up and nobody was around him.

The Great Dane and Bigfoot Brothers were all walking ahead of him with backs turned. He bent down and picked up the sling and walked back to the cliff and threw it into the river. He mumbled to himself, "Bigfoot," and smiled as he resumed counting his paces toward the triangle rock.

While he was peeing in a secluded spot behind a tree the helicopter pilot watched the detective throw the evidence in the river.

23

The Hawk-Eye View

WHEN THE CHOPPERS RETURNED to the field by the sheriff's department, news crews were surrounding the perimeter of the landing zone. Three police officers were also waiting at the landing zone. When the choppers set down, all the passengers waited for the blades to come to a complete stop before exiting. When the Bigfoot Brothers stepped down from the chopper, detective Stewart placed his hand on Billy's elbow and said, "Officers, arrest these boys and read them their Miranda rights! I've got this one!" Stewart squeezed Billy's elbow and reached up to Billy's neck with his other hand and swung him around to the chopper, almost banging Billy's head into the side of the chopper.

Detective Stewart grimaced and said loudly, "You have the right to remain silent!" And then in a whisper just loud enough for Billy to hear he said,

"I'm very excited to take a lot of pictures of you at the station." Then continuing loud again for all to hear, "Anything you say can and will be used against you in a court of law!" Billy's face turned angry red instantly as he futilely tried to pull away from Detective Stewart. Detective Stewart hit a pressure point on Billy and commanded, "Stop resisting!" The news photographers clicked away!

Rather than load them into the police cars, Detective Stewart had the officers walk them right through all the news crews and the quarter of a mile down the street to the front office of the police station. The press went crazy like rabid beasts, elbowing and shoving each other and running ahead along the path.

As they led the brothers into the station, Detective Stewart whispered into the district attorney's ear. The district attorney turned around smugly and took center stage at the top of the police station steps.

Anticipating the questions everyone had been asking and shouting during the long walk, he said, "Ladies and gentlemen, today the Bigfoot Brothers' deception comes to an end! They took us far into the mountains. They shared a fantastic story about being attacked by a whole group of bigfoots. They claim their friend, Eric Grimes, was murdered by the bigfoots and then buried in a grave. They took us to the grave where they said their friend was buried!" Milking the drama, he said, "There was indeed, a grave full of bones! The medical examiner has taken these bones as evidence to undergo further testing. But he assured me that he was one hundred percent positive that the bones that they led us to were in fact . . . deer bones! Today, I am charging the Bigfoot Brothers with impeding a police investigation, obstruction of justice, and murder!"

The Great Dane was still standing in the doorway behind the district attorney. He couldn't help himself; he made faces and stuck his tongue out during the whole announcement until the district attorney said, "deer bones" and then he stopped and turned pale as though someone had punched him in the gut.

When the district attorney finished, the Great Dane went inside and told the boys the recovered bones were deer bones and not to talk to anyone without him present. Adam turned and threw up.

"How?" Billy said to himself.

Daniel, in a trembling voice said, "Jail is not chill!"

"I'll protect you!" said Charlie.

The Great Dane's eyebrows raised and he quickly said, "I will see you tomorrow!" and turned and walked outside.

He scanned the scene searching through the crowd of news crews still milling around the steps, preparing to do breaking news reports for the five o'clock news. He spotted who he needed sitting on a bus stop bench to the right of the bottom of the steps. It was Robert Hawk.

He walked down the steps and plopped down on the bench next to him. "You have been a step ahead of the police and all these other reporters the last couple of days. How would you like exclusive access to the Bigfoot Brothers throughout this sham of a trial?"

"Yes! Yes! Yes!" said Hawk exuberantly.

"There is only one condition," said the Great Dane sternly.

"Anything!" said Hawk.

"You must always and only portray the boys as innocent, even if all the other media say they are guilty. Are you in?" asked the Dane, as he searched the steely blue eyes of Hawk.

Robert paused, thinking. and then said, "Yes, on one condition!"

The Dane squinted and let out a gruff, "What?"

"Buy me dinner at Randy's right now!" said Robert.

The Great Dane smiled and said, "Let's go eat!"

At six o'clock, Robert Hawk went live from inside the Bigfoot Brothers' house. He shared their family background as the camera zoomed in on family photos. He highlighted how the oldest brother, Adam, had become the lone guardian of his younger brothers when he was only seventeen after their mother died from brain cancer. He shared how they had opened up the B.A.G. Store together and how their friend Eric was as close to them as they were to each other.

Hawk closed the report by saying something terrible had happened to the Bigfoot Brothers and their friend Eric. They told the truth and now the district attorney is maliciously prosecuting them for the murder of Eric Grimes without a dead body, a motive, any eyewitnesses, a murder weapon, and a vast amount of reasonable doubt.

He signed off by saying, "The way I see it, with my Hawk-Eye vision is that there is every reason to let these fine brothers go and no reason for an expensive trial! You may have reasonable doubts about the existence of bigfoot. These boys had a million other options for stories they could have made up to tell the authorities, but they didn't. They told the truth because they believed beyond a reasonable doubt that bigfoots killed their friend.

"Since I wasn't there, I can only ask, 'What if it's true?' If the mysterious possibility of bigfoot causes us to doubt their guilt, then I believe we should find them innocent. If the district attorney proceeds with this case, I will be here bringing you exclusive interviews with the Bigfoot Brothers! This is Robert Hawk bringing you the Hawk-Eye View, from Pine Springs, the home of the Bigfoot Brothers and possibly bigfoot!"

Within ten minutes of the broadcast, Hawk's producer called and said, "You did it again! All the national news stations are calling asking for your piece for their 10 p.m. and 11 p.m. news broadcasts and their morning shows, too!"

Robert Hawk said, "That's great boss!"

The Great Dane was sitting in the leather recliner in the corner scribbling away on his legal pad. He dropped his pen, looked up, and said, "Keep doing that, and we will win this trial without even stepping foot in the courtroom if that D.A. knows what's good for him.

"You guys can stay here until I can get the boys out of jail. The arraignment will be Monday, so hopefully the bail will be low and I can get them out. You two can sleep in Charlie and Daniel's room. I will take Adam's room. Nobody bother Billy's room; he might have booby traps set up." Robert Hawk laughed. Dane shuffled down the hall and yelled back, "No, I'm serious! Stay out of Billy's room! Good night."

24
United

A FEW HOURS LATER, in the dark of cold jail cells, voices talked back and forth. They rehashed through the events of Eric's death.

Adam said, "All I can figure is the bigfoot ate Eric, but then put deer bones in the grave with his bloody, tattered green shirt as psychological warfare to keep us afraid. Maybe they ate him bones and all and then the Boss had the idea about the grave so they killed a deer and used its bones."

"The Great Dane will get us out of this mess!" Charlie said trying to keep everyone positive.

"He sure put that district attorney in his place at the site today! The Dane is chill under pressure!" said Daniel with a forced smile.

"Hey guys, here is some perspective for you; at least we have beds and food and God and each other!" said Adam.

Then Billy's voice, attempting to sound like Eric, echoed through the dark. "Oh yeah! Well, here's another thing!"—and he farted!

In unison they all yelled, "Eric!"

Adam chuckled first and then Charlie and Daniel joined in, followed by Billy's cacophonous laughter, which set them all off into full-blown laughter.

All the other prisoners on their cell block started yelling, "Shut up!" with other colorful descriptors added to their pleas for extra emphasis.

Though the brothers were in separate cells, the brothers felt the same solidarity that had been established in their brotherly bond since their mom had died. They would face the coming days united as one, just as they always had.

25
Reaping And Sowing

THIRTY MILES AWAY, HIGH in the mountains, shirtless Eric lay curled up, shivering with bigfoots lying down all around him. The old Gray Hunchback and the Boss were leaning with their backs against a large tree twenty feet away, peering at the human with unblinking red eyes. The hairy figure on Eric's left adjusted positions in its sleep, flopping its arm above its head, placing its armpit just inches from Eric's nose. Gagging and blowing air out of his nose, Eric rolled over to face the other way. As he completed his turn, a fart erupted from a matted hairy black butt right in his face. Eric quickly shifted to lie on his back, coughing and looking up at the stars saying, "Seriously?" He stared up at the stars pensively for another moment and then raised his brow as revelation filled his brain and said, "I guess you do really reap what you sow!"

Do not be deceived: God cannot be mocked. A man reaps what he sows. - Galatians 6:7 (NIV)

Do not be deceived: God cannot be mocked. A man reaps what he sows. - Galatians 6:7 (NIV)

26

Gold Diggers

A BALD, SLIGHTLY HUNCHED, wiry old man in black spandex shorts and a faded army-green tank top put his hand on the door handle of the Gold Digger's Donut Shop and pulled it open wide with an exaggerated grunt. He winked at the Laotian woman behind the counter and said, "Gold Diggers, sound off!"

A voice shot back from the corner table next to the window, "Chief Gold Digger present and accounted for!"

"Home-run Johnny here, still swinging my bat, coach!" came from a pear-shaped man in a Hawaiian shirt at the same table.

The spindly man at the door guffawed and said, "It's not time for little league, Johnny; Crazy Joe wants to see the gold!"

The Chief stood up as Crazy Joe marched over to the table and leaned across bringing his face just inches from the big Chief's chest where a gold nugget the size of a nickel was glued to a piece of wood and hung around the Chief's neck by a leather strap.

"Woo-eee! You're rich! Buy me a donut!" pleaded Crazy Joe.

The Chief smiled and said, "Only if Khamla has a bigfoot donut."

Crazy Joe straightened up and did a sharp military about-face, and marched up to the counter and confidently said, "I'll take a cup of coffee and a bigfoot donut."

Khamla handed him a paper cup and pointed to the carafe to the side of the display case, then handed him a paper plate with a bear claw on it and said in broken English, "Bigfoot not real! You pay for this!"

"Just one time, when you're making these bear claws, can't you just elongate this heel to make it into a bigfoot donut so it looks like a bigfoot footprint?" asked Crazy Joe.

"No! Then you make my husband pay and we lose money!" said Khamla. "You pay now! We like take you money! Haha!"

Crazy Joe squinted his eyes and said, "Your husband's a real gold digger!"

Khamla laughed and said, "That why I marry him! He have a big nugget!"

"Whoa, whoa, whoa!" Crazy Joe said as he shuffled away with his coffee and his bear claw. "Too much information!"

Khamla wiped the counter mumbling to herself, "Everyday, same thing! Crazy old man!"

At the table, the discussion quickly turned to the trial. Johnny held up the newspaper and said, "Paper says they expect both sides to give closing arguments this week."

"They're gonna find them guilty. People still don't believe in bigfoot!" said the Chief.

Crazy Joe countered, "They don't gotta believe in bigfoot, they just gotta believe the brothers."

Johnny asked, "Can they find them insane?"

"No, they didn't plead innocent by reason of insanity, so their mental condition isn't to be considered," answered the Chief.

"They didn't come across as crazy—not really," said Crazy Joe, staring at his coffee.

"You're an expert at that!" said Johnny.

Crazy Joe smiled and said, "That's why they call me Crazy Joe! I could've been their expert witness!"

Chief's hand reached up and touched the nugget on his necklace and said softly, "We all could have!"

Johnny said, "I can't relive what we went through again and share it with all those people! It's taken me years and a lot of donuts to learn to live with this PTSD."

"I know, I can't risk losing my business!" said the Chief.

Crazy Joe said, "Well, depending on what happens, I think I'm gonna tell the Bigfoot Brothers everything!"

Johnny stood up and said, "Oh, boy!" as he stepped away from the table.

Crazy Joe asked, "Where are you going?"

Johnny looked at him anxiously and said, "I'm getting another jelly donut!"

Crazy Joe leaned back and said, "Well, all right, stud!"

The Chief pointed to the small television hanging in the opposite corner and said, "Khamla, turn that up, please!"

Khamla found the remote and raised the volume level.

"Robert Hawk here with the Hawk-Eye View, coming to you live from outside the Pine Springs courthouse. Closing arguments took only one hour this morning in the Bigfoot Brothers' trial. Now it's all in the hands of the jurors. The prosecution painted a picture of a fight breaking out between hothead Billy and the Bigfoot Brothers' employee Eric, who is still missing and presumed dead.

"They speculated Eric was on top of the triangle rock and Billy went after him. Eric, scared for his life, stabbed Billy in his hand multiple times with a sharpened stick as he tried to grab him. Their theory continues that angry Adam was trying to convince Eric to come down and was struck in the head by a rock thrown by Eric. Adam lay unconscious on the ground and as the brothers ran to Adam, Eric tried to escape. But Eric, aware that the fittest brother, Charlie, would catch him easily, stabbed Charlie in the back several times and then turned to run. That is when, it is proposed, that Billy picked up the rock that was thrown at Adam, and hit Eric in the head, killing him.

"The prosecution then proposed that the Bigfoot Brothers conspired to cover up the death by concocting a story about a bigfoot attacking them in order to get away with it. Their motive? Publicity for their dying business. They claimed they escaped by outrunning a bigfoot.

"This was the weakest part of the defense's story, and the prosecution showed that a bear is as fast as a quarter horse and that no person could outrun a bear. The Bigfoot Brothers claimed they had a forty-yard head start, but the prosecution showed that even with a forty-yard head start, they could not outrun a quarter horse or a bear in a one-hundred-yard dash.

"The prosecution finished strong by showing photos of the river where the Bigfoot Brothers claim to have jumped off a forty-foot cliff into a boulder-laced river. The fact that not a single one of them was injured from this incredible jump was presented as unreasonable and unbelievable. In essence, the prosecution's closing argument proposed their own story, claiming that it is more likely and reasonable than the Bigfoot Brothers' mystical bigfoot story. The prosecution charged the jury to decide which story was more reasonable to believe.

"The Bigfoot Brothers' attorney, G. Dane, started his closing argument by showing family photos of Eric and the Anderson brothers. He demonstrated that they were practically brothers. To counter the prosecutor's proposed motive, he then pointed out that they did not seek out publicity and had no control of the media's reaction to their story. They never once contacted the media to discuss bigfoot.

"He made the strong point that they only came up with the idea to sell Bigfoot Brothers' merchandise after a certain reporter named Robert Hawk coined the phrase Bigfoot Brothers and tourists swarmed their shop asking for t-shirts. G. Dane said, 'Any money they have made has gone to pay for their very expensive and dashingly good-looking lawyer.'

"He closed his defense strongly by claiming this case doesn't actually come down to which story you believe—but that this case actually comes down to which storyteller you believe. He asked, 'Is it more reasonable to believe the Anderson brothers who never contradicted each other a single time in any of their accounts of what happened? Or, is it more reasonable to believe the district attorney who shared a story which he freely admitted he concocted in his mind?'

"So, viewers, it all comes down to this . . . will the jury believe a district attorney who makes up stories instead of providing evidence? Or, will they believe four brothers who honestly shared what they experienced, risking ridicule, reputation, and their freedom? What will the jury decide to consider? Story verses story or storyteller verses storytellers? One thing is for certain, . . . when the jury reaches a decision, I will be the first to bring you the entire story with my Hawk-Eye View!"

Crazy Joe announced, "Their friend is still out there! They need to know he is alive!"

The Chief speculated, "He might be! My people's legends say the hairy man would kidnap people. They didn't do it for food. Our legend says they might have bred with humans."

Crazy Joe and the Chief looked at Johnny. Johnny's eyes caught their questioning stares, "Don't look at me that way! I didn't get raped by those things when they had me! I think maybe they wanted to learn our language. Whenever I said something, they would try to copy the sound of my words. Some could even copy the sound of my voice and some words! They didn't like it when I refused to talk . . . They had ways to make me talk when I didn't want to."

"Oh! That's why you didn't talk much when we got you back!" said Crazy Joe remembering.

Johnny said, "It changed me!"

The Chief said, "If the Bigfoot Brothers didn't kill one of the bigfoots violently, then the bigfoots wouldn't kill Eric violently."

"No, but they might let him die slowly of starvation though!" said Johnny.

Crazy Joe said, "Is that why you got fat?"

"I guess so! I never pass up food or a meal because you never know if it will be your last! Do any of you remember what my last meal was before they took me?"

Crazy Joe shrugged. Johnny looked at the Chief inquisitively. The Chief's eyes squinted as he searched through sixty-five years of memories. Johnny sucked the jelly out of his donut with a slurping noise as usual.

The Chief's eyes got big and a smile slowly crept across his face as he blurted out, "You ate a smashed jelly donut!"

Johnny laughed.

Crazy Joe said, "That's right! You pulled that thing out of your back pocket after you sat on it!"

Johnny smiled and said, "When they had me, I promised myself that if I ever got home, I would eat a jelly donut every day for the rest of my life!"

The Chief called out, "Khamla, give Johnny another jelly donut on the house!"

"What about me?" asked Crazy Joe.

Khamla yelled, "No! You pay!"

Crazy Joe looked at Khamla and scrunched up his face and then stuck out his tongue. She started scolding him in Laotian and started shaking her towel at him.

Crazy Joe slapped the table and said decisively, "If the Bigfoot Brothers get out, I'm going to tell them where to find their friend!"

"They will probably just think you are a crazy old man!" said the Chief.

"Well, I've always been crazy, so I better not stop being crazy now! After all, I have a reputation to maintain!" bragged Crazy Joe sticking out his bony chest as he walked to the door. When he passed the counter on his way to the door, he looked back over his shoulder at Khamla and wiggled his butt and slapped it at her as he walked out.

27

Waiting

THE BIGFOOT BROTHERS OUTDOOR Store had been packed with people since the Bigfoot Brothers' story went national in September. Usually, the businesses in Pine Springs slowed down after Labor Day, but during the trial, the town was full of tourists every weekend. Every cabin, bed-and-breakfast, and hotel was sold out. All the restaurant's cash registers were ringing non-stop. In the Bigfoot Brothers' store, tourists were almost mob-like looking for Bigfoot Brothers t-shirts and asking questions about the Bigfoot Brothers. A ragtag crew of local eccentrics hand-picked by Adam's ex-girlfriend Sky staffed the store.

Sky had broken up with Adam the day after the Bigfoot Brothers were arrested and paraded down main street to the police station. Sky claimed she wanted publicity as a model, not an accused murderer's girlfriend. At least that is what she told Adam, but then when she left the jail she called a tabloid and sold them details about Adam and the Anderson brothers for ten thousand dollars. Her photo appeared on the cover of the tabloid with the caption, "Bigfoot Brothers' Girlfriend Tells All!" The same day the tabloid released the story, Sky left the small town of Pine Springs to pursue her modeling career.

The bail for the Bigfoot Brothers was set so high that they decided to stay in jail rather than risk losing their house. Luckily for Adam, one of the eccentrics hired by Sky before her departure was a former roadie for a grunge rock band. He went by the name of Wild Bill, and he was a marvel at selling T-shirts. Adam made him the manager of the store.

Wild Bill's party attitude and lifestyle kept the Bigfoot Brothers' Outdoor Store employees laid back and relaxed even when the store had wall-to-wall people in it. With Wild Bill's creativity, the store sold a literal ton of T-shirts. For the first time since the Anderson brothers had opened the business, the store had earned a decent profit for three months straight. Enough money was made to pay the store's overdue lease payments and cover their attorney, G. Dane's initial retainer fee.

With lots of time to think in their cells, the Bigfoot Brothers decided that if they won their case, they would keep the store open and use the Bigfoot Brothers brand to build their adventure guide business by offering overnight adventures for short three-mile hikes into the forest to a very popular overlook with spectacular evening views of the stars and the town of Pine Springs.

It would be far enough away from the town to make inexperienced hikers feel like they were in untouched wilderness, yet close enough to Pine Springs to make Adam and the brothers able to relax and not fear the hairy tribe of beasts that they had encountered twenty-five miles away in the forest. They figured if they lost the case, they could keep the store open and sell T-shirts that said, "Free The Bigfoot Brothers!"

With the closing arguments completed, the Bigfoot Brothers were all on edge in their cells, pacing like hamsters on spinning wheels in their cages. They felt like they had a fifty-fifty chance of winning the case and gaining their freedom. The last words of advice from the Bigfoot Brothers' attorney G. Dane was swirling in the brothers' minds. The Great Dane had told them that if the jury decided in one day, it would be a "guilty" verdict, but if it lasted beyond that, the jury was probably split and debating, which meant it could go either way.

So, waiting longer was good, but it felt like they were waiting to be hung from the gallows with nooses already snugly fit around their necks. They knew that soon the jury would pull the lever to open the trapdoor below their feet, and only then would they know if the ropes on their necks would break or if their necks would break.

Sixty-three hours after the jury began their deliberations, the phone rang at the jail summoning the Bigfoot Brothers to the courthouse.

28

The Delivery

At 10 a.m., on December 15, guards marched Adam and the Bigfoot Brothers into the courtroom. They were dressed in their court clothes. They all wore khaki pants and blue dress shirts buttoned tightly around their necks with black neckties tied with full-Windsor knots pressed firmly against their Adam's apples. The courtroom was packed tightly with people wedged into every seat, like a Super Bowl crowd.

The four Bigfoot Brothers stood for the reading of the verdict. The greasy-haired judge, like a salivating grim reaper, asked in a raspy voice for the verdict to be read out loud. The foreman of the jury stood and clasped the paper in his hands, like his hands were on the lever of the trap doors of the gallows. Many words were read, but all the Bigfoot Brothers heard was, "Not guilty." The words seemed to bounce off the wooden walls of the courtroom and echo above the erupting roar of the crowd.

Outside on the steps of the courthouse, reporter Robert Hawk stood in front of the cameras with the Bigfoot Brothers and the Great Dane and asked them, "What is next for you now that the trial is over and you are free?"

Adam answered, "We have a business to run! But I do dream of going gold panning in Alaska."

Then Hawk asked, "Will you all continue to guide people out into the wilderness even though there are big hairy monsters out there?"

All of them said, "Yes!"

Except Billy who said, "Heck, no!"

Shocked, Adam asked, "What about our plans?"

"I'm good with the plans we made, but I'm not going back into the woods!" replied Billy.

"Who is going to cook for our clients?" asked Charlie.

Daniel spoke excitedly, "I'll cook vegetarian!"

Adam and Charlie yelled, "No!"

"We'll talk later" said Billy as he pushed his way down the steps through the throngs of fans, reporters, and cameras.

The Great Dane cleared his throat and in the voice of a seasoned orator, looked to the rolling cameras and said, "Don't you people recognize a rehearsed publicity stunt when you see it? The Bigfoot Brothers are free and back in business; after all, they have some huge lawyer fees to pay!"

Everybody laughed and the crowd surged and engulfed the brothers. Fans were crowding and asking for autographs while reporters were asking questions and cameramen were elbowing people around them, while simultaneously trying to take steady pictures of the celebrities.

Charlie and Daniel posed together for a few pictures and answered a twin question they had heard a million times before. The question was, "When one of you gets hurt, does the other one feel it?" Charlie laughed and answered quickly by saying, "Yes! Somebody hit Daniel and I'll show you!" Daniel laughed.

The next question was a surprising twin question they had never heard before, "When you look at each other does it make you feel weird?" Daniel quipped, "Yes! When I look at Charlie's face, I get sick to my stomach!"

Charlie laughed and said, "Touché!" They pushed through the crowd to the bottom of the steps where Billy was waiting with the car.

The Great Dane and Adam were still at the top of the steps. Adam was answering questions and doing his best to use the phrase Bigfoot Brothers Outdoor Store as many times as he could. He hoped the free publicity would help them continue making good profits in the store through the winter.

After the twins entered the car, Billy started honking the horn for Adam. The people who had followed Charlie and Daniel to the car seeking autographs turned and ran back up the stairs toward Adam like ravenous autograph hounds.

Nobody noticed the little, skinny, hunched old man at the bottom of the steps in the back of the crowd. He was stalking Adam as he walked down the steps, biding his time for just the right moment. When Adam stepped off the bottom step, there was a blur of black spandex and army green. In a flash, the old man was on the cement holding his arm and rolling around howling in pain.

The old man had stepped in front of Adam, colliding into him like a master con man hitting his mark.

Adam responded by reaching to help the old man get up off the ground saying, "Are you okay? I'm so sorry! Are you okay? I didn't see you! I'm so sorry! Are you hurt?"

As Adam bent down to help up the old man, Crazy Joe winked at him and said, "I'm fine, young feller, but your friend isn't! Take this!" He extended his hand to Adam with a folded-up note. Adam took it and put it in his shirt pocket.

The Great Dane stepped in between them and said to Adam, "That was a masterful fake fall and this guy is probably going to sue you now."

Adam looked at the old man who was walking down the street away from him with a tall Indian on his left and a pear-shaped man in a Hawaiian shirt on his right. They were patting the little old man on his back like he had just robbed a bank. Adam shook his head and ducked into the car.

Pulling the crinkled note from his pocket, he read the scrawled sentence out loud that said, "Your friend is still alive and I know where he is!" It was signed "Crazy Joe" and had a telephone number.

The Great Dane said, "Whatever you do, don't call that number! That is a con man who is trying to tell you what he thinks you want to hear to suck you in, and then there will be a catch for you to give him some money to get information about your friend's location. Or, you will call him and he will ask you to pay him for the injuries he just suffered when you "deliberately" knocked him down, or he will threaten to sue you! Whatever you do, don't call that number!"

Adam ripped the note into strips and then into little pieces of confetti and threw them on the floor. Adam smiled and said, "Well if he sues us now, he can get half of the bill we owe our expensive lawyer!"

29
Crazy!

THE BIGFOOT BROTHERS OUTDOOR Store stayed busy throughout December and January. People only bought T-shirts, but that was enough to make the lease payments, restock the T-shirt inventory, and pay the Great Dane the rest of the money they owed him from their trial. There was a palpable difference in the attitudes of the town's people toward the Bigfoot Brothers.

The Bigfoot Brothers had grown accustomed to being whispered about, but now something was different. They were met with angry looks by the locals rather than the usual polite social greetings. The relatable Rockwell paintings of small-town American life could have all been actual scenes in Pine Springs before the Bigfoot Brothers' trial, but now something was amiss.

In February, the mayor asked them to attend the city council meeting. They showed up at the meeting at six in the evening, the exact time the mayor had asked them to be there, only to walk into the room in the middle of people yelling and shouting at a microphone about how their town had been ruined by the Bigfoot Brothers.

After the Bigfoot Brothers came in and sat down, every person stepped up to the microphone, turned around and yelled directly at the brothers rather than address the mayor and city council. The mayor tried to calm the crowd by explaining how the town's tax revenues had been through the roof and that the last year was the best financial year of the town's entire history in large part due to the Bigfoot Brothers' trial and publicity.

The crowd responded by chanting in unison, "We want our town back! We want our town back!"

Adam and the brothers left the building during the first minute of the chanting. Ten minutes later, when the chanting wouldn't subside, the mayor ended the meeting.

In March, the city council passed a new sign ordinance for businesses that required wooden signs and not banners. This was the first of a long series of new ordinances with large fines attached for code violations that only seemed to be enforced against the Bigfoot Brothers Outdoor Store. The city practiced selective blindness toward the other businesses in town, but tunnel vision on the Bigfoot Brothers' business.

The mayor became the loudest vocal opponent against the Bigfoot Brothers at every public meeting and every newspaper interview he gave. Although the town was hostile toward the Bigfoot Brothers, the tourists were not. Tourists kept coming to the town in droves. Every hotel desk, restaurant, and shop were under a constant barrage of tourists with questions about the Bigfoot Brothers.

In June, the Bigfoot Brothers Outdoor Store received a letter. "Care of Adam," was written across the envelope. The letter said, *"Your friend is still alive and I know where he is! I can help you rescue him! There are three commandments you will need to follow if you want to save Eric. #1. Guns are our friends; bigfoots are not! #2. Airborne is better than infantry! #3. You're not as crazy as Joe, until you believe what he knows!"* It was signed "Crazy Joe," and had an address. Adam threw the envelope in his junk drawer.

By July, the Bigfoot Brothers' T-shirt sales had slowed significantly. But the city's assault of fines had increased. They were a month behind on their store's lease and the landlord had received a letter from the city questioning the zoning and building code of his property. No tourists had purchased any overnight adventure trips with the Bigfoot Brothers all summer. People liked to ask questions and hear about bigfoot, buy T-shirts, and take a few photos, but they didn't trust the Bigfoot Brothers.

Adam dropped the price of the overnight trip from one hundred dollars a person to sixty dollars a person and then in desperation, down to forty dollars a person. He was wondering if he offered it for free if anyone would go. Then in the middle of August he received another letter, but this time, a courier had delivered it. After he opened it, Adam called all the brothers together for a back-room meeting at the store.

The letter was a legal notice of a civil suit that had been filed against Adam, Billy, Charlie, and Daniel for negligence and the wrongful death of Eric Grimes. Adam called the Great Dane for a consultation before he called everyone together for the meeting.

At the meeting Adam broke the news to everyone that they were being sued by Eric's father, and that they would likely lose and have to pay anywhere from $500,000 dollars to $1,000,000 in damages, not including their lawyer fees. He shared that they were going to close the store and currently owed $2,000 dollars in overdue rent. They had a new $353 fine from the city due to their new wooden sign on top of the building being three inches too tall.

After a moment of silence, Billy said, "Well it looks like we have a choice to make!"

Adam gave Billy a dejected look and said, "What's that?"

"Remember what you said to me in the cave? We choose to fight or we choose to die!" said Billy.

"Eric has already died!" whined Adam.

Billy raised his voice, "No! Remember what you said in the cave? Choosing not to fight is the same as choosing to die. So, the choice is simply this: WE FIGHT! Or WE DIE! And I'm not dying! No money means no food, and no food means starvation! Remember, cooks don't die of starvation! It will not happen! We are going to fight everyone! We'll fight the landlord! We'll fight the city! We will fight Eric's father! And we will fight all the bigfoot in these mountains for killing Eric and bringing all this misfortune upon us! The entire town thinks we're crazy! So, we might as well fight like crazy maniacs since they think we are crazy anyway!"

Billy's passionate speech mesmerized Charlie and Daniel. When he finished, they started applauding. Not to mock Billy, but because they agreed with everything he said.

Adam shouted, "Crazy? . . . Crazy? . . . Yes! That's it! . . . Crazy! We are crazy!"

Adam ran upstairs into his office and started searching frantically through the stacks of papers on his desk. Then he opened his drawer and started pulling out papers, glancing at them and tossing them onto his desk as though he was looking for a certain paper. Worried, sensitive Daniel followed Adam up the stairs and was watching from the doorway.

"Chill out, Adam, you're gonna have a heart attack!" said Daniel. Adam laughed crazily and said, "I wish!" as he continued his frantic search.

Charlie yelled up the stairs, "What are you looking for?"

Adam's eyes looked wild as he smiled, laughed, and shouted, "Crazy!"

"Looks like you found it!" mumbled Daniel.

Adam clutched an envelope tightly in his fist and lifted it up in the air above his head like he had won the lottery.

Pushing past Daniel, he ran downstairs and yelled, "Sell everything in the store for 70% off, I want it all sold this week! Sunday will be the last day of business and then we'll meet back here again next Monday at 8 a.m.!"

He ran out the back door of the warehouse, leaving it flung wide open. They all stood there in silence, stunned by Adam's weird behavior.

Daniel broke the silence by asking, "Guys, you know what next Monday is, right?"

Charlie shook his head no, but Billy looked at Daniel and said, "Labor Day?"

In a solemn voice, Daniel replied, "Remember Eric died last year on Labor Day? Next Monday is the one-year anniversary of Eric's death!"

They heard the squeal of tires and a spray of gravel hit the exterior metal wall of the warehouse as though Adam had lost all of his stoic marbles.

30

Crazy Joe's House

ADAM DROVE FIVE MILES out of town and turned onto a dirt road that led to the dump. After four miles of dust and gravel, he neared the end of the road. He noticed that there were small piles of junk scattered along the left side of the road in the last quarter of a mile. He figured the junk ended up there after people went to the dump and didn't have enough money to pay the dump fee, or maybe they drove out to the dump only to find it closed. This was the most likely explanation since the dump was only open on Saturdays and Thursdays. People just dumped their stuff as they were driving away from the locked gate.

He slowed his vehicle as he neared the locked gate to the dump at the end of the road and made a left turn on a small dirt road that veered off into the forest. On a pine tree, a faded green street read

Skunk Weed Lane. Underneath the street sign was another sign that said, "No Trespassing, Violators Will Be Shot!" The bullet holes in the sign seemed to add extra validity to the warning.

He drove two miles of snaky, unkempt road that had bushes and branches encroaching on the sides of the road. Periodically, Adam's truck seemed to emit long metallic whines of agony as the branches violated its paint job.

The road ended at a brown log cabin with a green roof. Adam tooted on his horn as he came to a stop, but he left the engine running in case a gun-toting home owner emerged firing at him. He saw the curtains in the front window move as though someone was peeking out. Ten seconds later the front door flew open and a woman emerged onto the porch with hands on her hips that seemed to say, "I'm ready to deal with you!"

Adam looked carefully to see if her hands were resting on six shooters like an old-west gunfighter before he turned off the engine and waved. She responded with an icy stare from hazel-green eyes. Adam felt something strange from her stare, like a surge of electricity had gone through his body. He instantly felt like there was some kind of cosmic chemistry in the universe activated at the subcellular level.

He got out of his truck and took a few steps toward the shack. A voice shot out, "You are the one!"

Adam stopped in his tracks and looked into her eyes. His heart surged. He noticed a strand of her long brown hair that had blown across her face and stuck to her lip, almost as if it was trying to get into her mouth to floss her straight white teeth.

"I feel the same way!" said Adam smiling.

"Huh?" she said, tilting her head to the left.

Adam clarified, "I think you are 'The One' too!"

"I did nothing to you! What do you mean, you believe, 'I am the one?'" she asked.

"I have faith that you might be the one that God has created for me!" replied Adam.

She grabbed a broom that was leaning next to the door and raised it to her shoulder like a baseball bat and said, "Don't count on that!"

Adam took a step backward and said, "Well what did you mean when you said, 'I am the one?'"

"You killed my Grandpa!" she said bitterly.

Surprised, Adam said, "Whoa, wait a minute! I don't even know your Grandpa!"

She continued, "You killed my Grandpa! You are 'the one' my Grandpa has been obsessing over for the last year! You are the reason my Grandpa walked off into the woods! You are the head Bigfoot Brother!"

By the time she finished, Adam had raised his hands up in front of him and was saying, "Whoa! Whoa! Whoa! Wait a minute! I don't even know your Grandpa!"

She threw the broom toward him hitting his shins and yelled, "Well, he knew you! Come in here and take a look at this mess! Oh, and by the way, there is no God!" She turned around and walked determinedly into the house.

He followed behind, limping into the house and mumbled, "God protect me!"

He stepped into a living room packed full of boxes packed with various items. On the coffee table, there were several rolls of tape atop a stack of unassembled cardboard boxes. Adam looked to the right to see a wall completely covered with Bigfoot Brothers newspaper articles nailed all over the wall. In the center of the wall were four enlarged photos.

Billy's photo had the words "The Cook" written in large red letters in permanent marker right on the wall under the photograph. Charlie's headshot was about six inches lower but next to Billy's photo with the words, "The Athlete" written under it on the wall. Another six inches underneath that photo was a large headshot of Daniel with a peace symbol drawn on the wall under it.

Above these three photos was a big photo of Adam with red letters above it on the wall that said, "The Leader." Pinned to the center of each of these photos was a piece of yarn that stretched three feet across the wall to the right and all met at a gigantic pin in the center of a large photo of Eric's face. The words "KIDNAPPED & ALIVE!" were written boldly underneath the photo and had been traced multiple times with a shaky hand.

Adam's eyes locked, paralyzed on the words underneath Eric's photo. About a foot higher on the wall above Eric's photo, there were about ten various size photos of a walking bigfoot. The photographs all showed the same pose.

The creature was walking, yet turning its upper torso sideways to look toward the photographer, almost as if it was posing like a model in a fashion show. This was the famous pose from the 16mm film shot in 1967 at Bluff Creek in Northern California. The sound of sobbing came from the floor to Adam's left.

He looked down to see the woman crying in the fetal position in the middle of scattered photographs and photo albums.

She was clutching a crumpled piece of paper in her hands saying over and over to herself, "This makes no sense!"

Adam knelt beside her and softly said, "What happened to your Grandpa?"

She handed him the paper in her hand. In the same red ink that was on the walls it said, "Dearest Wendy, I'm going to Nose Rock and then on to get Eric, the employee. Don't worry! Love, Crazy Joe."

On the back side of the paper was a drawing of a nose with two triangles above it. The top triangle had an X in it. "This is the note he left and then he walked into the mountains," she said, handing the paper to Adam.

Adam looked at the scrawled words on the wrinkled page, and familiarity grabbed his brain. His hand shot to his pocket and pulled out the envelope he had retrieved from his desk. He opened it and examined the handwriting, "Your friend is still alive and I know where he is! I can help you rescue him!"

"How long has he been missing?" asked Adam.

She began, "The last time I talked to him on the phone was on my birthday, August 16th. He acted very strange and said something about how he had been waiting for my birthday to come so he could go on his secret mission. That was the last day me or his friends heard from him.

"I came here to check on him on Monday, August 19, after he missed his usual Sunday phone call to me. I found the house like this. He left the back door wide open and I found his robe out in the woods behind the house. The police came and looked at the note and the house and said he seemed to be delusional or having a break with reality and that he possibly walked out in the forest to die peacefully, as a suicide mission.

The search team combed the woods five miles behind here for three days and then called it off. They said if he was out there, he would be dead by now. Then they said that it is also possible he just went on a trip and didn't tell anybody."

Adam looked at her with conviction and said, "No, he definitely went into the woods and I know where!"

Her watery eyes looked up.

"My brothers and I are going there next Monday," said Adam.

"Where?" she asked.

"Nose Rock," answered Adam.

"If that is an actual place, then I am going with you!" she said determinedly.

"No way! It's too dangerous!" declared Adam.

"Consider it our first date!" she said, wiping the tears from her face.

Adam smiled, "Okay! See? Faith pays off!"

"We ain't getting married, just looking for my Grandpa!" she said.

"Don't worry, I have faith that our first date will lead to a second date," said Adam confidently.

"No need to get excited, because I don't see that happening," she said flatly.

"Oh, that's okay. I walk by faith, not by sight!" said Adam undeterred. "Since we are going on a date, can you tell me your name?" asked Adam.

"My name's Wendy, preacher man," she said with a very slight smile.

31

The Meeting

AT 8:20 A.M. ON Monday morning, Billy, Charlie, and Daniel were at the store assembled in the back warehouse, waiting for Adam to show up to the 8 a.m. meeting he had asked them all to be on time for. Billy had tried to leave at 8:05, but Daniel had talked him into just sitting down in a comfortable reclining camping chair and chilling out.

When Billy said he didn't know how to chill, Daniel had him close his eyes and then starting directing him in how to calm his mind through contemplative prayer. Billy was reclined with his eyes closed and breathing rhythmically for about thirty seconds before Charlie signaled to Daniel by pointing to a couple of rolls of duct tape.

At 8:07, Billy was completely duct taped to the camping chair and screaming his head off.

By 8:10, Charlie and Daniel were across the room with Nerf guns. They took turns trying to shoot a plastic water bottle taped to a baseball hat on top of Billy's head.

By 8:15, Charlie and Daniel had taped a bullseye onto Billy's chest.

At 8:20, when Adam and Wendy walked into the back door of the warehouse, Charlie and Daniel were standing ten feet in front of Billy with Nerf guns raised and foam bullets flying. Billy had a paper cup filled to the rim with water balanced on top of his head. They had placed sunglasses on Billy to protect his eyes. Billy was trying to yell threats at them without moving his lips, like an angry ventriloquist.

Adam yelled, "Stop!"

Charlie and Daniel turned around reflexively firing in his direction. Wendy ran agilely to her left, leaving Adam to face the barrage of bullets.

When Charlie and Daniel saw that a woman had run away from Adam, they dropped their guns on the floor and started yelling, "Sorry! Sorry!"

"What are you doing?" yelled Adam.

Totally focused on the good-looking woman, Charlie and Daniel ran over to her and introduced themselves, apologizing. Adam went over to Billy and removed the water cup and sunglasses from his head.

Angry, Billy yelled, "Set me free, Adam! Set me free!" but as he was saying it, he was leaning his head to the side to see around Adam and shoot daggers from his eyes into the backs of his brothers.

"Calm down and then I will cut you loose!" said Adam.

Wendy was laughing hard and said, "Oh, I'm fine! But Adam's been shot and may need medical attention!"

Charlie and Daniel turned around and said, "Sorry, Adam!"

"What are you guys doing?" asked Adam.

Billy yelled, "It's your fault, Adam!"

"How is all this my fault, Billy?"

Billy rolled his eyes and said, "You were late! I tried to leave, and the twins tricked me! If you were on time like you usually are, none of this would have happened!"

"I'm sorry things are crazy now and they are about to get crazier!" said Adam.

"There you go again using that word, crazy. Maybe you are the one going crazy! I'm calm; now let me loose!" demanded Billy.

"Promise me you will not go after Charlie and Daniel right now and I will let you go?" proclaimed Adam. He knew better than to ask Billy to forget it completely.

"Okay, not right now!" said Billy. Adam cut Billy loose.

Billy got up from the chair and looked at Charlie and Daniel. He took a step toward Charlie and Daniel and sneered while he dragged his extended index finger across his throat. Then he coughed as he turned, walked over to the kitchenette and grabbed a big plastic cup and filled it with ice and water.

Adam announced, "Guys, this beautiful lady is Wendy! Everyone, please sit down and let's begin this meeting."

"About time!" said Billy as he sat back down in the recliner with his large cup of ice water with a straw in it. Wendy, Charlie, and Daniel grabbed some camping chairs and sat next to Billy.

Adam began. "We have to get crazy! If we don't get crazy, we will lose everything and be in debt for the rest of our lives. We are all trapped in this situation, just like we were by the bigfoots when we were in the cave. All the people in town are mad at us. The mayor and the city council are against us. The tourists don't trust us enough to go in the woods with us, and our T-shirt sales have almost stopped.

"Eric's drunk, abusive father is suing us and will win a massive judgement against us. We are losing the store and everything. So really, we have nothing to lose.

"Maybe you all remember when I got handed a note after the trial by an old man."

Billy interjected, "You mean the guy you knocked to the ground?"

"Yes, that guy!" confirmed Adam.

"You knocked him down?" asked Wendy angrily.

"Yes, but he bumped into me and faked a fall! He was fine! He just wanted to hand me a note. The note said, 'Your friend is still alive and I know where he is!' It was signed, 'Crazy Joe.' I ripped it up in the car. Well, Crazy Joe is Wendy's grandfather."

The brothers said, "Oh!"

Adam continued, "He sent me another letter in June. The letter said, 'Your friend is still alive and I know where he is! I can help you rescue him!' Well, last week I went to his house to see what he knows, and it turns out he has gone into the woods by himself to get Eric."

"Wait a minute! Is this the guy the Search and Rescue Team looked for last month?" asked Charlie.

"Yes!" answered Wendy.

"Do you really think he is still alive?" whispered Charlie.

"I don't know if he is still alive or not, but I know where he went!" said Adam.

"Like the letter says, he went to look for Eric!" exclaimed Billy.

"Yes, but what I mean is, I KNOW the location where he went to look for Eric because he left a map."

Getting agitated, Charlie said, "That would've been helpful information for us on the Search and Rescue Team!"

Adam grabbed a marker and drew a nose with two triangles above it on the whiteboard. "Here is the map," Charlie.

Looking at it, Daniel said, "I don't think that is a very helpful map."

A look of recognition came over Billy's face and he said, "Oh no! You ARE crazy! I ain't going there!"

Charlie and Daniel looked at Billy and asked, "Where?"

Adam tapped the marker on the board and said, "Crazy Joe called this 'Nose Rock.'"

Billy continued, "I ain't going back there!"

Wendy started to cry.

Charlie said, "Oh, I see."

Daniel said, "Wait a minute, you mean, that nose drawing is the triangle rock in the meadow?"

Adam nodded. Billy put his hand on Wendy's shoulder as she started sobbing harder.

"If that nose is triangle rock, then the two triangles above it must be mountains?" observed Daniel.

"Yes! Exactly!" said Adam, "And this top one, with the X in it, is where Crazy Joe is going. This is where he thinks Eric is."

"Joe really is crazy!" said Charlie.

Wendy sobbed loudly and said, "He is crazy! He has always been crazy! They have called him Crazy Joe since he was a kid and he and his friends went into these mountains and came back talking about hairy monsters that took their friend. They claimed they fought the hairy beasts and rescued their friend.

So, is my Grandpa crazy? Yes! But he has never once lied to me in my entire life! He is about as crazy as you all, who claim to have fought bigfoots at the triangle rock!"

Wendy raised her eyebrows and asked, "Are you all liars?" All the brothers shook their heads no.

Wendy responded, "So, what I want to know is, are you crazy Bigfoot Brothers going to go after my crazy Grandpa or am I going to have to go after him by myself?"

When she finished, tears were gushing out of her and she was leaning her head onto Billy's arm, sobbing uncontrollably.

Billy gave in, "Okay, okay, I change my mind! I am crazy, too! And I am going to Nose Rock! Stop crying!"

Charlie looked at Daniel and then said, "Count us in!"

"I know this map isn't much to look at, but we will have to walk by faith and not by sight. We will put our faith in Crazy Joe, go back to Nose Rock, and on to this second mountain to try to find him," said Adam.

Wendy wiped her eyes, stood up, and looked at Adam and asked, "When do we leave?"

"Today, in about two hours! Go get your stuff together and we will meet at the helicopter pad behind the fire station!" answered Adam.

A piercing scream emitted from Charlie and Daniel, who involuntarily reacted to the drenching attack of ice-cold water flying onto their backs from Billy's large cup. This was immediately followed up with the cup flying through the air, like a missile. The cup ricocheted perfectly off of Charlie's face and into Daniel's chin before it fell to the ground.

Wendy ran nimbly toward Adam, as Billy flung aside his camping chair and started charging towards Charlie and Daniel. The twins screamed and ran out of the warehouse with Billy huffing close on their heels yelling, "Payback time!"

Wendy asked Adam, "How in the world did you guys survive in that cave without killing each other?" Adam smiled and winked and said, "Faith."

32

The Donut Shop

WENDY LEFT THE WAREHOUSE and drove straight to the donut shop. She had all of her backpacking gear already loaded in her trunk and she thought she should go tell the Gold Diggers what was going on. When she entered the donut shop, Johnny was at the front counter sporting his favorite Hawaiian shirt taking a bite out of the jelly donut in his right hand, while trying to sort the change in his left palm using only his left thumb. When Wendy walked in and said, "Gold Diggers, sound off!" Johnny looked up at her and dropped all hIs change on the floor, saluted, and said, "Home Run Johnny still sitting the bench!"

From the corner by the window a low voice said, "Chief Gold Digger staying on the reservation!" She had grown up hearing the roll call every time her Grandpa brought her into the donut shop. Wendy laughed and smiled at her Grandpa's old friends, not understanding their guilt-laden responses to the roll call. The Gold Digger's leader and friend, Crazy

Joe, had gone on a dangerous mission and they had refused to join him. Now they were wondering what had happened to him, and they were grieving.

Khamla got up from the corner table where the Chief was sitting and said, "Hello, Wendy! You still like chocolate donuts with sprinkles?"

"How sweet, Khamla; you remembered! But do you remember what I like to drink?" asked Wendy.

"You sit here; I bring it; you see!" answered Khamla.

Johnny blocked Wendy's path to give her a one-armed hug and then started picking up his coins. Wendy slid into the booth across from the Chief. Khamla brought her a chocolate sprinkle donut and a hot chocolate topped with a tower of whipped cream with colorful sprinkles on top.

"This the famous Wendy Special!" said Khamla, setting it down in front of Wendy.

"You got it right!" exclaimed Wendy, laughing.

"Are you going back to Los Angeles?" asked the Chief.

"No, not yet, but I am going on a trip. That's actually why I'm here. I thought you would want to know since you are like family. There has been a new development," said Wendy.

"Did they find his body?" asked Johnny as red jelly dripped from his donut on to his shirt.

"No, not yet, but I might have a better idea where to look! Have you guys ever heard of a place called Nose Rock?" asked Wendy.

Johnny let out a whimper and looked away.

The Chief said, "We know it well!"

"I'm going there today with the Bigfoot Brothers," declared Wendy.

"No! You can't!" protested Johnny.

"But Crazy Joe left a map, and that is where he went!" said Wendy.

"You mustn't go!" protested Johnny.

"The Bigfoot Brothers are harmless!" said Wendy.

"It's not them we are worried about—it's the bigfoots!" said the Chief.

"Do you really believe all that?" asked Wendy.

"They took me when we were kids and Crazy Joe got me back!" said Johnny.

Wendy stared blankly at Johnny's and the Chief's faces, seeing the genuine fear in their eyes.

"He left a note and a map that says he has gone to get the employee! The map shows Nose Rock and the two mountains past it!" explained Wendy.

"That's where they had me! . . . He really went?" said Johnny.

"I didn't think he was serious," mumbled the Chief.

Wendy erupted, "Wait a minute! You both knew he wanted to go there? And you didn't stop him? You didn't call me? You let him go alone into these mountains? You believe there are dangerous monsters in these mountains and you let your leader and friend go alone? You could have called me! You should have called me! You could have stopped him!"

Distraught, Johnny said, "If we knew for sure he was serious about this, we would have stopped him! You have to understand, none of us, including him, have ever gone back into the mountains since we were kids! We didn't believe he would really do it! We're all seventy-five years old."

"When he stopped coming in here, we thought he was just playing a joke on us! I thought maybe he went on a three-day cruise or something. But then he just didn't come back. We realized he probably actually went into the mountains," said the Chief.

"Did you call the detective?" asked Wendy.

"Yes, and he said there's no way a seventy-five-year-old man could survive this long in those mountains," answered the Chief as he broke down crying.

Wendy put her hand out and through her own streams of trickling tears, said, "I'm going to go look!"

"Take this for luck!" said Johnny as he reached in his shirt pocket and pulled out an old pocket knife with the letters G.D. carved onto the wooden handle of the folded knife.

The Chief reached up with his big hands and took off his gold nugget necklace and put it on Wendy, saying, "Put this back on the mountain. If Crazy Joe is up there it should be with him!"

Wendy smiled and said, "He sure did like this nugget!"

She waved as she pulled out of the donut shop parking lot and tried to imagine what Johnny and the Chief would have looked like as kids, and she tried to picture Crazy Joe as a kid standing there with them. She watched them look at each other and turn and walk back into the donut shop.

33

Return to The Cave

Adam was waiting at the launchpad at 11 a.m., looking at his watch. By 11:15, everyone but Billy had arrived and met the pilot. At 11:20, Billy sauntered up casually and looked Adam in the eye and said sarcastically, "Sorry I'm late; things have been Crr-aayyy-zeee!" Adam shook his head and said, "Load up!"

In another fifteen minutes they were at Nose Rock, unloading off the chopper. Adam handed each of his brothers an extra day pack to carry. Before walking away from the chopper, Adam spoke with the pilot and handed him a fat wad of money. The pilot handed him a large, yellow duffel bag.

Adam waved goodbye to the pilot and said, "Quick, let's get to the cave in case they are coming!" They turned and followed Adam, but kept their heads on swivels as they walked.

When they climbed up into the cave, they saw a small single burner backpacker's stove with an empty can of chili on it. Sitting next to it on the ground was a plastic grocery bag with a variety of hot chili peppers in it.

Wendy picked up the pepper bag and said, "I don't believe it! Crazy Joe has been here! My grandpa has been here! My grandpa is alive!"

"Are you sure it was him?" asked Adam.

"My grandpa always carries a bag of peppers in his pocket," said Wendy.

Billy asked, "Why does he carry peppers? Is it because he is a cook?"

"No, that's not it," answered Wendy, "Joe claims they are the secret to his success."

Intrigued, Daniel asked, "Was Crazy Joe successful?"

Wendy looked at Daniel and cocked her head to the side and said, "Yes! He was a very successful failure! He failed at every scheme he ever tried in his life! And believe me, he tried a lot of crazy, get-rich-quick schemes. He was always talking about getting rich! He would always refer to himself as a gold digger. In fact, he and his friends all called themselves the Gold Diggers and Crazy Joe was the leader of their group."

"Well, at least we know we aren't on a wild goose chase," said Adam.

"I can't believe he made it this far!" said Charlie.

"Me either!" said Wendy.

"I gotta meet this guy!" said Daniel.

"Okay, at least we know which direction he went," said Adam. "But finding him is still going to be like finding a needle in a haystack. Remember he has been out here a full eighteen days now and he is seventy-five years old. He couldn't have possibly carried enough camping or survival supplies with him." Everyone's eyes looked down at the cave floor as those words sank in.

Daniel reached over and put his hand on Wendy's shoulder and said, "He made it this far; maybe he will surprise us!"

"There is a little more to the letter he sent me," said Adam, "He gave us rules."

Adam took the letter out of his pants pocket and read, "Commandment #1: 'Guns are our friends; Bigfoots are not!' So, we need to assume Crazy Joe has a gun! In each daypack I gave to you, you will find a 9mm handgun."

"Do you really think a bullet could stop the Boss before he ripped us to pieces?" asked Billy.

"It may not stop him, but maybe it will slow him down enough for me to outrun him!" answered Adam.

"That's pretty slow!" quipped Billy.

Adam laughed, "Ha!" and continued, "Commandment #2: 'Airborne is better than infantry!' I don't know what this means; does anyone have any ideas?"

Billy asked Wendy, "Was Crazy Joe in the military?"

"No, he tried to sign up during Vietnam, but they said he was too short and skinny and they thought boot camp would kill him," answered Wendy.

"Well, look at us now, we are up here in this cave off the ground and that was probably the only reason we survived last time. I guess this could be what he meant by that," proposed Charlie.

Adam conceded, "It looks like he was here, so maybe you are right. This airborne commandment also got me thinking about air drops. A military infantry marches in and they carry their supplies with them, but if they have air support, they can have supplies dropped off at strategic locations! So that is what I have planned.

"We will have two strategic supply drops. Each of you has a map in your day pack with the locations marked. One will happen tomorrow and one will happen Wednesday. Each drop will be a large yellow duffel bag or two and will have weapons, ammunition, and food. So, we have added airborne support. This is probably not what he meant, but if we run into these things, I want all the firepower we can get!"

Daniel spoke up, "First of all, where in the heck did you get all these guns? You know I don't like guns."

Billy had his 9mm out in his hand and was pointing it towards the top of Nose Rock and said, "Well, I don't like getting eaten by bigfoots! I'll take Daniel's gun! Besides, everybody knows: guns don't kill people; bigfoots kill people!"

Charlie and Billy laughed.

Adam growled, "No! Everyone needs a gun!"

"Where is my gun?" asked Wendy.

"You are with me," answered Adam.

Wendy glared at him and said, "Give me a weapon now or leave me here alone . . . oh great protector!"

Adam looked at her and sighed and said, "Fine! But you have to carry the pack!" and he tossed the seventeen pound pack to her.

Wendy caught it and saluted and said, "Yes, sir!"

Adam continued, "Commandment #3 says, 'You're not as crazy as Joe, until you believe what he knows!' The question is, *What does Crazy Joe know?* He claims he knows where Eric is, and he claims Eric is still alive! And here's the crazy thing. He doesn't just claim it. He obviously believes it! I'm sorry guys, I just don't believe Eric is still alive! We all heard them tear him a part! We all saw his shredded bloody clothes!

I think Crazy Joe is delusional, but then again, that's what the whole town thinks about us!"

"We are definitely crazy for coming back out here!" said Billy.

Adam continued, "We are absolutely crazy, but maybe not quite as crazy as Crazy Joe! . . . No offense, Wendy!"

"Oh, none taken; he's totally crazy!" she said confidently.

"So, we are keeping two of Crazy Joe's three commandments for success," said Adam.

"Great, we are only 66% as crazy as Joe and we are following his psycho manifesto," mumbled Billy.

"Why are we wasting time talking?" asked Charlie impatiently.

"We kind of needed to stay up here in this cave a little while to see if the bigfoots saw the chopper and came to get us!" said Adam.

"Oh yeah," said Charlie as he looked out of the cave to the tree line.

"We all need to look at the maps in our day packs and talk about the drop location. Everyone, get out your maps," said Adam.

Adam continued, "Today we are going to hike about three miles to higher ground and then we will fortify that position if possible. You will see today's camp marked by the small square next to the number 1 on your map. That square is a half mile from the drop zone that is marked with a star. It is close to the drop zone, but not too close. I want us to be at the drop zone tomorrow morning at 8:00 a.m. We will be there waiting in the tree line so when the yellow bag drops, we can grab it and run. The drop will happen at 8:00 and I want to be out of that area by 8:01. I don't want to be there if the bigfoot come to investigate.

"Just in case we need it, I planned for a second supply drop at the drop zone for Wednesday morning. Oh, and one last thing. If things go bad and somehow, we get separated, we will all try to reconnoiter back at the drop zone. If you get there and nobody shows up after an hour, make your way back here to this cave and look in the duffel bag. He held up the yellow duffel bag and then wedged it in the back corner of the cave where the jawbone from a fox skeleton was sitting. In your day packs there is a walkie talkie with a headset. If we need to use them, we will be on channel five. Remember! Use channel five, to stay alive! Let's get going!"

34

Base Camp One

BY THE TIME THEY made it to the first base camp, it was four o'clock. "Let's get ready for the night. We aren't going to have a fire so we don't need firewood," commanded Adam.

"How am I supposed to cook?" asked Billy.

"Do you want every bigfoot in the area to know you are here and run over here like moths to a flame?" asked Adam rhetorically. "No! You can eat protein bars, trail mix, and water!"

Exasperated, Billy said, "You can eat that, I brought my little single-burner camp stove and some cans of beans and coffee; I gotta have coffee!"

"Then why are you throwing a hissy fit about a campfire?" asked Adam.

"Well, if they show up here tonight in the dark, shouldn't we have a pile of wood ready to light to keep them from coming in here and grabbing us?" asked Charlie.

"We are going to fortify this camp with a perimeter trip wire so that doesn't happen. I brought fishing line and hand grenades!" explained Adam.

"Where in the heck did you get hand grenades?" asked Daniel.

"I can't explain that now. We have to get this done while we still have daylight," said Adam.

"Well, you thought of everything for this first date, didn't you?" mocked Wendy.

Daniel gave her a funny look and said, "You guys are dating?"

"That's what he calls this," said Wendy.

"No wonder he is still single!" said Daniel.

Wendy laughed.

"Don't worry, Wendy, I'll grow on you!" said Adam.

Billy mumbled, "Like a wart."

They set up a thirty-yard perimeter, placing the trip lines six and a half feet up in the air, connected to trees. Anything that moved toward them and was taller than that would walk into the line and pull the pin on the grenade attached to the tree. They had used an entire spool of fishing line and twelve grenades. They finished setting up the twelfth grenade in the last seconds of daylight.

"Let's get back to camp and talk about tomorrow," said Adam.

"Talk-Smalk! I'm eating beans!" announced Billy.

"Gonna be music later tonight!" said Charlie.

"Eat with me, Charlie, and we'll have a symphony!" invited Billy.

Wendy laughed and said, "Count me in!"

"Girl's fart?" asked Daniel, surprised.

"No, of course not! They toot!" said Wendy. "Consider me the horn section in the symphony."

"Adam can be our audience!" said Billy, laughing.

Adam shook his head and said, "You guys are out of control!"

Control was one thing Adam worked hard at. He always had a plan and strategy for everything. The world inside his head was filing systems full of blueprints for maximum success with minimum loss. He thought over every possible outcome before he made a choice. He carefully weighed the pros and cons. And then after he had done all of that, he went over it again in his mind, step-by-step, to see if he had overlooked anything.

By the time he shared a plan with anyone, he had already thought through the three best plans and the challenges each presented and decided on the best course of action. This pensive quality made him very confident as a leader, some might say rigid. But he was exactly the kind of decisive leader you would want to follow if you are going into battle!

Adam laid out the next day's itinerary. They would break camp at 7 a.m. and get to the first drop site a half mile away from them by 7:30. They would wait concealed in the tree line until the 8:00 drop.

They would get the package and exit the drop site at 8:01 to begin their trek down the backside of the mountain. They would make another fortified camp on a forested slope a quarter mile west of the edge of the large valley that sat between the two mountains. Adam had figured the downhill hike would be quicker than the previous day's hike and might take a few hours or less. He figured they could have their next camp fortified by 2:01 p.m. He planned for them to spend the rest of the afternoon scouting the surrounding area for signs of bigfoot.

Wednesday's plan was simple. They would climb to the top of the second mountain to look for Crazy Joe. They would be heavily armed in case they came across any angry bigfoot. Adam wasn't sure they would find Crazy Joe, and he was certain they wouldn't find Eric. But Adam knew his biggest fear was possible and much more likely. His biggest fear was that they would find the tribe of bigfoots led by the Boss, who would seek to end their lives. These mountains belonged to them.

Two questions were haunting Adam. The unknown answers became a driving force in him: *What did Crazy Joe know? Why was he in these mountains?* It didn't make any sense for a seventy-five-year-old man to hike into these mountains alone. *Was he really crazy? Or did he actually know something about Eric?* The only one who could answer these questions was Crazy Joe. Adam decided to proceed with the mindset that Crazy Joe was still alive and making his way to the top of the second mountain, or perhaps he was already there. Adam would follow.

35

Crazy Joe's
Recon

CRAZY JOE WAS RIGHT. The bigfoots were in the same place they had been so many years past. They even had a sentry posted in the large tree. It was the same large tree Crazy Joe had climbed so many years ago to see into the camp when he came for his friend Johnny.

Crazy Joe had moved into his vantage point just at the fading light of dusk on Saturday, September 1. He spent two full days watching them to make sure he knew their daytime schedule.

He had positioned himself very carefully in the center of a very large patch of thorny blackberry bushes on a hillside about a hundred yards from the sentry tree. He had carefully crawled into the patch on his belly, following a small rabbit trail into the bush. To his great surprise, he was skinny enough that he barely got stuck at all by the thorns.

On his first night, a bear came by the bush to eat some berries for the entire night and then wandered off just before daylight. Crazy Joe didn't sleep that night, worried that he might snore and the bear might investigate.

Both days, the sentry was perched in his position in the tallest tree from just before sunrise until a hunting party would return to the camp. The hunting party was made up of two large brown males and a red female. Each morning around 8 a.m., they would come walking out of the forest, crossing the meadow toward the sentry as they returned.

Each time they returned, they carried live animals with them. The first day they had two raccoons and the second day they had a rabbit and a fox. Crazy Joe wondered why the animals they had hunted were still alive. He decided the tribe must only eat really fresh meat or blood. Maybe they did it so parasites or maggots wouldn't get into their bodies.

Next, Crazy Joe would hear noisy commotion coming from their camp for a few hours. He would hear rumbles and roars, wood knocks, and eventually, dying animal death squeals, followed by multiple weird high-pitched screams. He called it the feeding frenzy. Usually after 11 a.m., the commotion would die down and the sentry would return to his lookout tree.

The rest of the day was usually quiet, except for a red female bigfoot and her young child's appearance. They would exit the camp and spend some time in the meadow, where the child would play. Each time before they entered the meadow, they would let out a whistle. The sentry would turn his head and slowly scan the area around the meadow. Then he would whistle back, seeming to answer them with an all-clear signal.

Whenever they left the meadow, the little one would let out a whoop and smack the base of the sentry tree as they passed by, and the sentry would answer back with a whoop and smack his chest.

Every afternoon about an hour before dusk the hunting party would leave the camp and cross the meadow headed back into the forest. About noon Monday, Crazy Joe made up his mind and decided he would sneak into the bigfoot camp Tuesday morning. If the schedule followed the same pattern, the sentry would be gone from his post after the hunting party returned. Joe planned to move into a new hidden position inside the bigfoot camp during all the noisy commotion of the feeding frenzy.

36

The Drop

When the helicopter buzzed over the drop site Tuesday morning at 8 a.m., the Bigfoot Brothers were waiting in the tree line at the edge of the small meadow. The yellow bag was shoved out of the hovering helicopter from an altitude of 150 feet and landed almost directly in the center of the meadow. The bag hit the ground with such force that the zipper broke and the bag ripped, spraying the contents into the tall grass. The helicopter circled the meadow once and departed. Adam sent Charlie and Daniel to retrieve the bag because they were the fastest runners.

When they reached the bag, they saw grenades on the ground and rifle barrels sticking out of the bag. Charlie grabbed the bag and turned to run, but two rifles fell out. Daniel picked up four grenades off the ground and started running back to the trees.

Charlie yelled, "Come back and help me!"

Daniel stopped and came back to the bag. He shoved the grenades into the torn hole in the bag and picked up one rifle off the ground and slung it over his shoulder and turned again to run toward the trees. But when Charlie picked up the bag by the handles, the bag ripped more and the grenades spilled out.

Charlie yelled, "Daniel, help!"

Daniel ignored him and just kept running. Charlie picked up the bag and ran to the trees with grenades falling out as he ran across the meadow to the tree line.

When he finally made it to the tree line Adam's exasperated voice yelled, "Everyone help pick up those grenades!"

Everybody entered the meadow and fanned out walking toward the center, collecting grenades like Easter eggs as they went. At 8:14, they were all standing in the center of the meadow. Adam checked his watch and sighed.

Wendy watched Adam look at his watch and said, "Well, nothing's happening here! Is it time to move yet? Can we go now?"

⸺⸺⊠⸺⸺

IN ANOTHER MEADOW ON the top of the next mountain, something was happening. The hunting party had returned at 7:57 and signaled the sentry with the usual whistle before entering the meadow and waited for the all-clear response. They walked through the meadow chattering and hooting, excited about something.

Crazy Joe saw what they were excited about, and said, "I guess they really like raccoon meat." The two brown ones were carrying four raccoons. By 8:06, the sentry had left his post and a ruckus of grunts, hoots, and whistles were rising through the morning's sunrays into the forest canopy.

Crazy Joe belly crawled out of the thorny blackberry bushes and ran across the meadow to the sentry tree. He peeked around it and saw nothing. He continued into the forest, dodging from tree to tree, moving closer and closer to the noise. He saw large, hairy figures up ahead through the trees, but his eyes were searching for a hairless body. He needed to get closer to see better—without being detected. He saw a sloping granite rock ledge beyond the creatures. He whispered to himself, "Time for the second commandment! 'Airborne is better than infantry!'"

Circling wide to his left, he made it to a clump of thick manzanita bushes growing at the edge of the rock ledge. He eased behind them and to the back of the sloping granite. He scampered thirty yards up the incline to a crack where two granite slabs came together.

He looked down into the crack and could see that the narrow opening at the top gradually widened as it descended to the ground. It was maybe fifteen feet to the floor. He guessed it was maybe twenty-four inches wide at the bottom, but only twelve inches at the top. He crawled on his hands and knees to the edge to peak over and get the bird's-eye view.

Looking down, he saw the activity happening in the clearing below. The hairy creatures had formed a large circle and hissing raccoons were scampering back and forth in the center of the circle. One raccoon was on the ground dead, but three others were running in circles snarling and looking for an escape path.

The bigfoots seemed to take turns throwing small rocks at the raccoons, trying to kill them with a head shot. Crazy Joe saw a shirtless human figure curled up ten feet to his left at the base of the rock face. He seemed to be asleep, but Joe noticed that his head was moving, watching the bigfoot play their game.

One of the bigfoots kept turning around and looking at the frail human every few minutes. Joe noticed the skeleton-like frame of Eric and he got an idea. He took a small mirror from his pant pocket and stuck his arm out over the edge to get the angle he needed to reflect the sunlight onto the face of Eric. With a slight move of his hand, he made the light dance on Eric's cheek and eye.

Eric raised his hand to block the light and sat up. When Crazy Joe hit his eye again with the glaring light, Eric looked up. He rubbed his eyeballs and looked again at Joe as though he was seeing things. Just then a bigfoot turned around and saw Eric sitting up. The beast took a step toward Eric and kicked dirt at him. Eric cowered and lay back down again, but this time he lay with his head to his right, putting him a little closer to Crazy Joe.

After the bigfoot turned away, Crazy Joe's head popped back over the ledge. Crazy Joe pointed at Eric and then pointed down to the bottom of the crack. He motioned for Eric to move to the crack. Eric checked to see if he was being watched and slid slowly inch by inch toward the crack. He was two feet from the crack and looking up at Crazy Joe when the bigfoot turned around again to check on him and saw he had moved. The bigfoot looked up to see what Eric was looking at and saw Crazy Joe's head.

Crazy Joe shrieked, "Airborne!" as he jumped up and off the edge and landed on the ground in front of the crack! The shriek startled the creatures, and they all turned to see two skinny bodies at the bottom of the crack.

The big one that had kicked dirt at Eric lunged, swinging his massive arm, but he was too slow. Two skeleton-like figures had disappeared into the dark recesses of the crack! The big one tried to reach into the small opening of the crack to grab a bony body, but the narrow crack was too small for him to reach his muscular arm in past his elbow. The creature looked into the crack and saw his prey looking at him from about nine feet back in the darkness. He let out a horrendous scream into the crack.

Crazy Joe yelled back at him, "Eat a Tic-Tac, sock breath!"

37

Base Camp Two

CHARLIE WAS LEADING THE group, bushwhacking a path down the mountain. Taking out his canteen, he took a gulp of water as he turned to look back up the mountain to see how far everyone was behind him. Most were looking down, paying special attention to their foot placement on the uneven slope. Daniel was the last person in line with a nice gap behind everyone else. His hiking rhythm was staying true to his personality—relaxed and enjoying the scenery on the journey.

Daniel's eyes, as though directed by some mysterious twin power, locked on Charlie's. Daniel's eyes widened as he yelled and pointed, "Bear!"

"Nice try!" Charlie yelled as he turned and took a step right into the backside of a huge cinnamon-colored black bear.

Charlie screamed and threw his open canteen at the bear as they both tried to back up and turn away and run in the other direction on Jello-ee legs.

Both feet and paws were shuffling frantically like they were on a soapy slip-n-slide. When Charlie's feet caught traction, his body launched back up the path and bumped right into Billy.

Billy yelled, "Watch it!" but then he saw the bear and turned to run up the mountain, yelling, "Crap!"

"Stop! It's gone!" yelled Adam waving his hands.

"Maybe that will teach you to listen to your younger brother!" said Daniel, laughing.

"At least it wasn't a mama bear with a cub!" said Charlie.

"Need to change your chonies, Charlie?" asked Adam, laughing hysterically.

"No, I'm not wearing any!" answered Charlie.

"Hey, remember there's a lady present, let's not go there!" said Billy.

"Relax, I wasn't going to show him!" said Charlie.

Wendy mumbled, "It's too early in the day for the moon to come out now!"

"Maybe the bear didn't want moon pie!" said Billy grinning at Wendy.

Hearing this, Daniel said, "I don't know. I think both Charlie and the bear did a pretty good moonwalk!"

"I thought you weren't supposed to run from a black bear or they would think you were food?" asked Billy.

"Charlie ran like fast food!" said Adam.

"That isn't supposed to happen to the guy in the front of the line! Predators go after the person in the back of the line!" said Charlie laughing.

"If that bear was going after you, you would be dead! I think you gave that poor bear a heart attack!" said Adam.

They were at the bottom of the mountain at 1:15 p.m.

Adam said, "Let's stick to the cover of this tree line and walk to the west around this valley until we hit the creek. Then we will follow it up the slope a few hundred yards and make camp."

"Are we going to Rambo it up again?" asked Billy.

"Of course!" said Adam.

Billy asked, "Can I cook?"

"No!" came Adam's quick reply. "No fire or Bunsen burners tonight!"

"Okay, I understand that, but if I can cook when we get there while you all set up the perimeter, we can all have a nice hot meal before dusk," suggested Billy.

Adam's stomach growled and he said, "Okay, that's fine! What are you cooking?"

"That's for me to know and you to find out!" said Billy. Charlie started guessing.

When they arrived at the spot, they were all hungrier than they should've been due to listening to Charlie list off food choices for thirty minutes straight. Adam directed everyone, and they set up a forty-yard perimeter with grenades and trigger lines six and a half feet up in the air again.

Adam wanted another perimeter set ten yards closer in from the grenades set up four feet off the ground, with a four-pound fishing line connected to some military-style perimeter alarms they strapped to trees. When something walked through the fishing line, it would pull the clip from the alarm boxes which would set off a 134-decible alarm and blink red, flashing lights. Adam hoped four feet off the ground would be low enough to catch a bear or bigfoot sneaking up on all fours.

When they finished the perimeter set-up they returned to the camp, famished. Billy was just putting chunks of cooked steak on wooden kabobs interspersed with bell peppers, red onions, and pineapple. Sitting on the fallen tree Billy was using for a counter, was a bubbling pot of black beans simmering on a little one-burner camp stove. Next to the beans were two slightly smashed foil-covered bricks of cornbread.

Everyone closed in on the food like a pack of hyenas, emitting excited animal-like noises as they ate. Billy enjoyed their noises of approval as much as he enjoyed the food.

When they all finished eating, Adam said, "Let's take a peek and see what is on the flat area on top of the next mountain."

"Dusk will begin in a few hours! There's no way we can hike to the top right now!" said Daniel incredulously.

"I don't want to march up that mountain now. I just want to see it! Remember Crazy Joe's commandment #2: 'Air Force is better than Army!' Let's get airborne?" said Adam.

Everyone was looking at him like he had totally lost his mind. He was feeling more and more comfortable being considered crazy and unpredictable by others. He was finding a freedom and power he had never known before. Adam reached in his pack and pulled out a drone and held it up.

38

The Deer

HIGH IN THE BIG tree above the meadow, the sentry yawned and extended his long arms to stretch but then froze halfway through his stretch, becoming as still as a statue. A deer and her fawn were at the far edge of the meadow slowly sauntering into the meadow. The rest of the bigfoot troop was spread out napping in the clearing near the granite rock face and crevice. The sentry knew if he whistled to wake the hunters, he would scare off the tasty ungulates. He would try to get them by himself.

Moving very slowly, he reached around the tree with his long arm and grasped the thick branch on the other side and slipped off his branch, swinging around to the other side of the tree. He climbed down the tree quietly. Once on the ground he lowered himself to all fours and peeked around the tree to see where the deer were. Then he crept, keeping his torso low to the ground, moving whenever the mama deer lowered her head to grab a mouthful of grass and freezing when she raised her head to chew and look around.

The sentry was within thirty yards when the mama deer saw him and quickly let out a terrified snort, raised her tail, and bound away into the forest. The fawn's reaction was too slow. At 4:23 p.m., the sentry walked into the center of the troop with the live fawn under his arm and let out a loud whoop. The troop woke and began chattering with excitement and formed a large semicircle in the clearing by the granite rock, trapping the fawn from escape.

Huddled inside the narrow and dark crevice between two granite rocks, a scruffy-faced being with stringy, gray hair extended a bony hand out into the daylight and gasped as though the sunlight was dissolving his pale wrinkled flesh. Dirty nails scratched at the air as a baby deer was being herded closer and closer to the crack. The fawn was backing away from the silverback beast standing in front of it.

The beast was leaning forward with its arms spread wide apart, waiting for the fawn to jump to the left or the right. The golden fawn with its back to the crevice was more petrified by the gruesome predator in front of it, than the wheezing sound emitting from the dark crack in the rocks behind it. The bigfoot in front of it let out a low growl, and the fawn took another step backwards. SNAP! A bony hand had grabbed its back leg and pulled and twisted hard. The fawn screamed!

The bigfoot in front of the fawn lunged forward and grabbed the fawn by the neck with one giant hand and pulled... POP! The torso of the fawn hung suspended off the ground in the tight grip of the Boss. It was missing a hind leg.

The silverback let out a frustrated scream that bounced off the granite rocks and echoed through the trees. In the crevice, an inhumane laughter and a smacking sound filled the dark void. A minute later, the flicker of a flame danced in the crevice's darkness. Soon the smell of cooking meat reached out from the crack, mocking carnivorous appetites.

The silverback stomped around, screamed, and threw a tantrum like a toddler who didn't want to share his cookies.

In the crack, a voice sang out, "You got big feet and I took your meat! I took your meat, and you got beat! My name is Crazy Joe, and I got the flow! Come at me again and I'll bite your toe! Ha, ha, ha, ha! What—What! Sucka!"

While the other bigfoots were ripping up the deer carcass, feeding on the flesh, the silverback tried to reach into the crack but could only fit his muscular arm in up to the elbow. A black-haired juvenile bigfoot with a red stripe down the center of its head and back watched as the silverback pounded the rock in frustration and turned around to walk toward the carcass.

A bone flew out of the crack and hit the bigfoot in the back of the head. The silverback roared and jumped back to the crack, trying another angry attempt to reach in. The ever-observant juvenile cackled and the hand of a large, reddish-brown-haired female reached out and hit him in the back of the head, letting out a grunt. The song started up again from inside the crack.

The silverback reacted with a roar and stomped his feet and slapped the ground with his open hands. He turned away and galloped on all fours into the trees. SNAP-CREAK-POP! The silverback returned running upright on two legs carrying a long tree branch. He ran to the crack and started stabbing the branch into the crack repeatedly with great force, as though he was spearfishing. The juvenile cackled loudly again but bobbed this time like a prizefighter as his reddish-brown mama's hand shot out again for his head.

In the back of the dark crevice, two skeleton-like bodies were laying on the ground next to each other back to back. The stabbing branch was searching the darkness to inflict pain. Now and then a wince would escape as the sharp end of the branch found some leg skin. Crazy Joe started to scream every time the branch stabbed the rock wall above them, hoping to make the angry silverback think he was hitting the right spot. It worked. After twenty minutes, the stabbing stopped.

Crazy Joe and Eric sat up and Joe whispered, "We will live another week off this meat."

"Maybe, if he doesn't kill us first!" said Eric.

"He won't kill us unless we kill one of them," said Crazy Joe confidently.

"How do you know that?" asked Eric.

"Oh, I know about these beasts. My friend Johnny was here when I was a kid and I got him out. How do you think I found you?" replied Crazy Joe.

"You came looking for me?" asked Eric.

"Well, someone had to do it! These things are smart, but we are smarter. Don't worry, we will escape," said Crazy Joe.

"I am ready to get out of here! I was about to kill myself when you showed up," confessed Eric.

"Why?" asked Crazy Joe.

"I'm tired of being their toy! They hit me and hurt me for amusement. They made me make noises and tried to copy me. For a while I thought they wanted me to teach them to talk, and I tried, but they are just animals. They can mimic the sounds they hear, but they comprehend nothing except emotion.

"They understand anger, laughter, sadness, pain, and maybe affection but they don't use language like ours to talk. They make clicks, grunts, chatters, and moans combined with subtle hand signals, body language, or facial contortions. And then, of course,

I was starving to death, but that's not even the worst part! The worst part is they stink! They stink really bad and it was killing me!" vented Eric.

Crazy Joe rubbed his hand on his chin and said, "Well, they won't try to kill you unless you kill one of them, or try to escape. But they will injure you for fun and let you starve to death."

"Yeah, that's how this happened," exclaimed Eric as he held up his hand, showing off a digit that had been broken sideways and healed that way.

"I made the mistake of trying to grab some meat from a kill like everyone else instead of waiting for them to throw their gristle and leftover bones to me!" said Eric.

"We ain't sucking on bones tonight! Let's have another piece of this meat; it's going to be cold tonight, and we got to build up your strength for our escape!" said Crazy Joe.

Outside the crevice, an excited single hoot came from the juvenile as he pointed to the sky. The rest of the bigfoot looked up and began hooting and running to the base of the trees. The silverback let out a howl that sounded like a firetruck siren. The sentry came running. High above the trees, a buzzing shape was hovering. Inside the dark crevice, there was movement.

First a head popped out and looked around and then Crazy Joe jumped out into the daylight and grabbed the long poking branch off the ground and then jumped back into the crack, pulling it in behind him. He fastened his green tank top onto the skinny, jagged end of the branch and hoisted it up so the makeshift flag poked up through the narrow opening above them. He began waving the flag back and forth and yelling, "We're here!" Eric joined in yelling, "Help us!"

39

The Drone

FIVE SETS OF EYES stared in unbelief at Adam's cell phone screen. Looking back at them through the screen were scattering bigfoot. Then a skinny pale figure emerged from within the rocks and then disappeared again. A few seconds later an army green flag popped out of the top of the rocks and moved back and forth violently.

Wendy said frantically, "That's my grandpa's tank top! That's my grandpa! Go closer!"

They watched the beasts emerge from under the trees into the opening. They were throwing rocks at the drone. The silverback ran around to the top of the rocks and grabbed the waving branch and yanked it up hard, wrenching it completely out of the bony, gnarled hands within the crack.

Wendy, staring in disbelief, said, "I can't believe they're real!"

"That's the leader. We call him the Boss," Adam said.

The Boss's massive arms swung the flag-branch like a huge baseball bat at the drone, barely missing. The drone jerked to the right. A lanky red female jumped off the rock and tried to grab the drone.

"That's the Red Zombie!" exclaimed Charlie.

The drone rotated just in time to see the black-haired juvenile with the red stripe throw a rock. The drone jerked to the left, lurching right into the trajectory of the rock missile thrown by the juvenile. The drone crashed to the ground, and the juvenile scampered to collect his prize.

"Hey, that was the Cup Thief!" announced Daniel.

A series of quick, vicious roars came from the Boss. He was flinging his cupped hands from his chest outward, splaying them towards the forest with each roar. The sentry and seven others answered with shrieking screams and turned and ran into the forest. The hunt began.

Wendy had tears streaming down her face, and she hugged Adam saying, "He's alive! Crazy Joe's alive!"

"Those walking hairy armpits have him trapped!" Billy said.

"No, you don't know my grandpa. He would tell you he has them trapped, but they just don't know it. My grandpa has a plan," corrected Wendy.

"Your grandpa really is crazy!" Daniel said.

"I'll take crazy over dead any day!" Wendy said.

Adam smiled. Wendy saw Adam staring at her and winked at him and mouthed the words, "Thank you!"

She was so ecstatic about her grandpa, she thought of what it would be like to thank Adam with a kiss, but they weren't alone. She began to think that maybe there was something to God and faith after all.

"I counted twelve bigfoots on that video," shared Charlie.

"We know where they are, and we have guns and grenades this time," said Adam.

"It's time for payback! This time we will hunt them!" Billy said.

"Hopefully, they will run when we shoot and we can just get Crazy Joe and leave," Adam said.

"Hopefully . . . Wendy, do you think Eric is still alive? I mean, I thought Crazy Joe was dead, but he's not!" asked Daniel.

"Well, let me ask you all one question?" Wendy said.

They all looked at her.

She continued, "Was your friend Eric as crazy as my Grandpa?"

"Yes!" the brothers replied in unison.

"Then, maybe he is alive with my Grandpa," Wendy said.

For the very first time, logical Adam believed Eric could actually still be alive.

Adam pushed the record button on his phone and said, "Let's talk about tomorrow's rescue. They have the higher ground. We will need to get them to move away from their camp and then breach their camp while it's less fortified. We need to control their movements."

"How in the world are we supposed to do that? These are wild beasts! You can't control a wild animal." Billy said.

"You are right, Billy; wild beasts can't be controlled, but they can be attracted!" Adam said.

"What are we supposed to do? Yell yoo-hoo, bigfoot?" asked Billy.

"You are on the right track!" said Adam. "Have you ever heard of a predator call?"

"Isn't that when you make a noise that sounds like an injured or dying animal and predators come to investigate and then you shoot them?" asked Billy.

"Yes, that's right!" confirmed Adam.

"Who's gonna be the bait?" asked Billy

Adam kept his gaze fixed on Billy and slowly smiled. Billy's eyes widened as he understood the unspoken implication, "NO WAY! I am NOT going to be bait!"

Adam laughed, "Yes, you are! But don't worry, so are all of us!"

Raising his voice in frustration, Billy said, "Yelling 'here we are, bigfoot; come and eat us!' doesn't sound like a brilliant plan."

"It will be our voices, but not us!" replied Adam.

"What are we gonna do, throw our voices like ventriloquists?" asked Billy.

"Exactly!" said Adam.

"Would ya please stop playing games, and explain, because the more you talk, the more I feel like the dummy in this scenario!" pleaded Billy.

"I am recording us talking on my phone, I am going to loop it and then we will place my phone and a Bluetooth speaker outside their camp to draw some of them away from their camp so we can launch a surprise attack on those in their camp guarding Crazy Joe," explained Adam.

"Misdirection?" asked Billy.

"Exactly!" said Adam.

THREE HOURS LATER, NINE hairy silhouettes were standing on the ridge line high above them. They were listening to voices floating up to the ridge top on the evening breeze. The sentry made a hand gesture, and the hunters began creeping down the slope.

40

The Hunting Party

ADAM SAT LEANING AGAINST the log with a brown wool blanket draped over his shoulders and his walkie talkie earpiece in his ear. Wendy was sprawled out flat on the ground next to him under a green blanket. The moonlight flickered through the gently swaying trees and danced on her hair, making the natural, lighter-brown strands in her hair look like blond highlights. Adam forced himself to stop staring at Wendy and moved his eyes to look at Billy but his heart seemed to stay locked on Wendy's beauty.

Billy was snoring twenty feet away. Adam thought to himself, *So much for sleep*. Charlie had hung a hammock between two trees and was sleeping like a baby in his mummy bag. Daniel was standing guard for the first two-hour shift of the night. He was patrolling twenty yards up-slope in the forest with his walkie talkie set to Channel five and an earpiece in his right ear.

⸻⋈⸻

THE HUNTING PARTY CREPT slowly down from the ridge, letting the voices in the wind help them zone in on the exact location of their prey. When they were a hundred yards away, the sentry went to all fours and the others followed his lead. In another thirty minutes, they were fifty yards closer and spreading apart to increase the distance between them to ten-yard gaps. When the voices and movement in the camp went silent, the creatures sat still waiting and listening. When the time was right, the sentry would signal the attack with a loud shriek.

Shortly after the voices subsided, a heavy irregular gurgling noise disrupted the night's silence. The noise gradually increased in duration and volume. Sometimes there would be a snort or cough, and then the silence would return for a while. But then the offensive assault on the silence would begin again.

The sentry wondered if it was a warning growl. He wondered if they knew they were there, not that it mattered. They would be no match for his brawn. The rest of the hunting party would herd the creatures toward him, and he would kill them all. In between the strange growling fits, the sentry could hear footfalls in the pine needles. One of the hairless creatures was pacing back and forth repeatedly. Judging from the sound, the pacing one was closer to them than the growling one. The sentry would kill him first.

———⋈———

WITH FIVE MINUTES LEFT in his shift, Daniel radioed Adam and said he was coming back into camp. Right as Adam put his hand on Billy to shake him awake for his shift, an inhumane shriek cut through the night air and down his spine. Immediately, an ear-splitting 134-decibel squeal and pulsing red light lit up on the mountain thirty yards above them to the right. Then another to the left. Then another.

Adam yelled, "They're coming!" Swiftly he turned to grab his 30-06 hunting rifle. The peaceful camp had gone from peace to chaos in a hundredth of a second. An exploding fireball lit up the night as a grenade exploded! The concussion echoed, bouncing through the mountains. Adam's adrenaline surged, contracting his blood vessels and redirecting his blood toward his major muscle groups and heart and lungs. His hands shook.

Adam tensely pointed his rifle up the glowing mountain lit up with pulsing red lights and fire. A dark figure moved! Adam's finger twitched uncontrollably in fear and his rifle muzzle flashed.

As soon as the echo of the gunshot left Adam's ear, Daniel's voice was screaming in his earbuds, "I'm shot! I'm shot!"

"Hold your fire, it's Daniel!" yelled Adam.

"That announcement's a little late!" came a shaky voice from the bush in front of them. Daniel crawled out of the bush awkwardly using two hands and one knee dragging the other bloody leg, yet he still moved quickly.

A barrage of screaming, angry shrieks and howls blasted down from the mountain.

Adam yelled, "Fire!"

They all spread out, screaming and howling back as they unloaded their guns, shooting toward the red glowing trees up the mountainside. The bigfoots' shrieks and howls stopped after the drowning noise of blasting guns claimed the airspace.

When the firing stopped, ten ringing ears strained to listen for movement in the forest while reloading guns. Daniel was lying on the ground next to the log, creating a puddle of blood from the rivers of blood streaming from the holes in his lower leg.

Charlie finished reloading the clip of his Glock 20 and ran to Daniel.

Daniel said, "Get my pack!"

From somewhere in the dark they heard low chattering mumbles and huffing grunts.

Billy pointed one of his guns and fired off five shots, screaming, "DIE, MONKEYS!"

"BILLY, STOP! SAVE THE AMMO!" yelled Adam.

Wendy moved to help with Daniel's wounds, "You're bleeding like a stuck pig!"

"Ha, ha, she just called you a pig!" said Charlie.

"Shut up, genius! Remember, we're twins," said Daniel.

"It looks like the bullet went straight through your calf muscle," said Wendy.

Sweat dripped off Daniel's head as he shivered and said, "I'm cold!"

"You're in shock!" said Wendy.

Looking to Charlie she said, "Cover him in your mummy bag!"

"I'll start a fire!" said Adam.

Billy stood firmly planted in between all of them and the forest, like a bodyguard, he clicked on his headlamp, shining it into the trees and bushes up-slope.

Confidently holding two fully loaded Glocks, he announced, "I ain't moving!"

A rock the size of a softball hit the ground in front of him hard and bounced.

He stepped backward bumping into Adam, "They're throwing rocks!"

Adam took charge, "Let's get next to the base of these trees so no rocks can drop on us from above. Instead of one fire in the center, we'll set a bunch of fires all around our perimeter. Come on, Billy; help me!"

Billy stuck his guns in his belt and said, "Let's light up this forest!"

Billy had only taken two steps when a rock conked him on the head. He went down hard.

41

The Perimeter

A STALKY, RED-HAIRED FEMALE with a body like a vending machine picked up the charred remains of the sentry's head and let out a long mournful wail. Two brawny brown soldiers were dragging what remained of the corpse of a medium-sized reddish-brown soldier over to her.

Dropping the cranium of her mate, she slapped the ground hard and screamed. The soldiers dropped to all fours. She moved forward slowly in a panther-like crawl, staying as low to the ground as possible. She slinked toward the closest squealing light. Getting to the tree, she pounded the pulsing red light, smashing the device into useless plastic shards. The others, taking their cue from her, moved to the other screeching glows and destroyed them.

She looked down into the camp. She saw one of her prey with a bright light shining from its head. She picked up a rock and flung it with a rapid underhand flick of her arm. The rock missed its mark, landing at the feet of her target. She picked up another rock as her victim shuffled backward a few steps. Her arm flashed faster this time, and she saw her prey fall to the ground. She let out another harrowing wail and the soldiers began a torrential downpour of rocks on the camp.

The angry, red-haired dowager moved closer. She could smell blood. Just twenty yards in front of her, flames exploded up into the sky. Deep within her an instinctual fear gripped her as she felt a wave of heat and light hit her face. Smoke permeated her nostrils, and she turned to crawl back up the mountain into the darkness. Something above her glimmered, catching her eye. Her eyes followed the horizontal luminescent thread over to a pine.

In the glow from the fire, she could make out an object. It was the size of a small pine cone, but it wasn't anything that grew in the forest. She rose to her full height to inspect it closer. It was level with her eyes. She tilted her head back and flared her nostrils to examine the scent, but instead, the acrid smoke blowing up the mountain assaulted her mucous membranes.

She raised her hand to smash the foreign object just as she had the red light. There was a loud boom from the camp behind her, and a hot piece of lead dug into the flesh between her shoulder blades. She screamed and fell to her knees.

A big brown soldier stood up and ran to her, stretching out his long arm. His fingertip barely grazed her shoulder when life ended for both of them. He hadn't even felt the pull of the fishing line that hit his throat and pulled the grenade's pin. The explosion sent red and brown body parts like shrapnel into the surrounding trees.

All the creatures chattered as they darted up the mountain, away from the noxious smell of flames and death. They would gather on the ridge and regroup. They would restrain their bloodlust until daylight. After sunrise, they would move to satiate their vengeance.

Down the mountain, seven fires burned, overpowering the darkness, but broadcasting the human's exact location. Firelight surrounded the prey. The only question the remaining members of the hunting party had was who would lead the hunt?

Five hunters remained. The largest was a tall mass of testosterone and muscles covered with dark brown hair. Slightly shorter but wider was a grey-faced beast with jet black hair. Next were two cinnamon-brown brothers the same height as the grey-faced one, but proportioned like smaller versions of the tall, dark-brown beast. Then there was the lanky, red-haired female. She was the shortest at a height of seven feet and weighed in around two hundred and fifty pounds.

Lanky-red moved to a tree with a twenty-inch diameter with loose roots at its base and chattered. The others spread out, finding their own trees all about the same twenty-inch diameter. The Red one shrieked, and they all leaned in and pushed hard against their trees. The lanky-red one's tree was the first to fall to the ground, making a loud boom just seconds before the tall dark brown one's hit the ground. All the trees fell, echoing like explosions across the mountain range, but Lanky-red's was first. It was decided. She would lead the hunt.

She let out a loud howl and set off a haunting chain reaction from a pack of coyotes down in the valley. She wasn't the biggest, but she was definitely the most cunning of the bunch. The bloodlust in her eyes projected there would be no mercy, but would be a singular, crystal-clear focus on killing. Blood would answer for blood. She would avenge her mother's death and she would enjoy it.

42
Gunsmoke!

AFTER BILLY WAS KNOCKED out and the hailstorm of rocks stopped. Adam knew the beasts would be coming. He saw one of the throbbing red glows go dark after a loud deep thud. Adam heard several more forceful thuds and the forest went silent and dark. Just twenty yards upslope from the camp, Adam touched his lighter to the lowest branch of a small six-foot pine; the flame popped as it grabbed hold of the dead needles. In another thirty seconds, it engulfed the entire tree in a sizzling fireball.

As Adam moved to his right to light another tree, he saw the illuminated back of a chunky, eight-foot red beast standing in front of a tree thirty yards away. He raised his rifle to his shoulder and fired. The creature fell to its knees, screaming. He saw a hulking nine-foot dark blur move toward the wounded one and the mountain exploded. The trip line grenade had disassembled both of the beasts.

He heard the distinct sound of sticks snapping and bushes moving as heavy animals moved rapidly up the mountain and away from them. He lit another tree on fire, and another, and another, until there was a half circle of seven burning trees between them and the creatures. Adam moved to Wendy, who was tending to Billy's head wound. Charlie had his guns pointed up hill as he sat next to Daniel.

Daniel was lying with his back flat on the ground with his injured leg propped up on a log. Blood was still trickling from the entrance and exit wounds.

Billy started bragging to Wendy in slurred words, "Get me some hot dog buns and wood sticks from your house and I will make you some delicious McDouble-McGriddle-McMuffins that taste exactly like McDonalds."

"Dang, Billy, you have a serious concussion!" said Adam.

Billy shouted, "You don't know that! You ain't a doctor! Only Dr. Wendy can tell me that!"

"Billy, you have always hated McDonalds! You refuse to eat McDonalds and now you brag you can cook almost up to their high standards? Something is wrong!" said Adam with worry in his voice.

"I'm just tired," said Billy as he closed his eyes.

Wendy slapped him. Billy opened his eyes and yelled at Adam.

Adam yelled, "Wendy did it!" and turned his back to look at Daniel's bloody calf.

Billy mumbled, "Wendy would never do that to me, I cook McDonald's for her!"

Wendy looked over at Daniel and then up at Adam and said, "We have to stop that bleeding!"

"Gunsmoke!" declared Adam.

Wendy tilted her head slightly to the left and gave him a quizzical look.

"I saw what to do on an old T.V. show... cauterization," answered Adam.

Adam stood up and went over to Billy's pack and ruffled through it. He pulled out a pair of metal bacon tongs and walked to a burning tree and stuck the tongs in the flame.

He came back to Charlie with the tongs behind his back and whispered in his ear, "hold him down!"

Adam slid the blood-soaked bandage down to Daniel's ankle and opened the red-hot tongs wide and grabbed Daniel's calf muscle like a biscuit, searing the bullet's entrance and exit wounds at the same time.

Daniel flailed his arms and screamed. A wide-eyed Billy copied Daniel's scream with full commitment, completely unsure why they were screaming.

When Adam released the calf muscle, Daniel passed out and Billy said, "Mmm, I smell bacon!"

They heard five loud thundering booms crashing from the top of the mountain.

"Well, at least we know where those things are right now!" said Wendy.

Adam looked at Wendy and then his brothers and announced, "You all have to leave now!"

43

The Retreat

"WHAT ABOUT MY GRANDPA?" asked Wendy tersely.

"I will get Crazy Joe," said Adam.

"You can't get him by yourself!" cried Wendy.

"I'm going to have to! We have lost the element of surprise. They know where we are! If we stay here, we will all die! While they are up that mountain you all can escape. They came looking for us and we have killed some of them. They are waiting for daylight and then they will come for us and they will kill us all. If you all leave right now, you will have a four-hour head start and you might make it to the cave before they catch up to you," explained Adam.

Wendy started to speak but Adam continued, "Charlie is going to have to practically carry Daniel and you will have to help with Billy."

"Billy will be fine; I will stay with you!" protested Wendy.

"Really? You think so? Look at Billy!" Adam said gesturing toward Billy.

Billy was arguing with his backpack, "You are a liar! Your pancakes taste like crap cuz you put salt in them!" He paused, hearing some imagined reply, "I do not use pepper! I use nutmeg in mine—that's the secret ingredient!"

"Okay, I see your point!" said Wendy. "He's crazier than Joe!"

"After those creatures discover that you are all gone, they will take off to follow you. When the coast is clear, I will leave my hiding place and go after Crazy Joe. They will never expect me at their camp!"

"Maybe you are as crazy as Crazy Joe, too!" said Wendy.

"Yeah well, it does appear that I am following in his footsteps right into the bigfoot camp!" replied Adam.

Charlie asked, "Where are you going to hide?"

"If I walk off and hide in the woods they might track my footsteps or something and find me so I am just going to hide right here!" reasoned Adam.

"Where?" queried Charlie.

Adam smacked the log and said, "Here! Hurry! Help me dig out a spot under this root ball and then you guys can cover it with branches and bush and make it look natural. Then you all need to leave!"

In fifteen minutes, they had dug a cave-like compartment under the massive root ball. Adam climbed into the hole with his rifle, backpack and two Glocks. In five more minutes, they had buried him under bushes and branches. They scattered pine needles all over their footprints around the root ball.

Charlie woke up Daniel and Wendy cleverly asked Billy to help her put on her backpack.

Billy happily said, "That's a great idea; you look cold!"

Wendy laughed and said, "You better put yours on too!" Billy eagerly complied.

Five minutes down the trail, they stopped and made a splint for Daniel's leg. The moon peaked over the tops of the trees, giving them light to hike by. They circled the edge of the valley and started up the next mountain toward the drop site. That's when it got hard.

Daniel could not push off his left calf, and a walking stick didn't give him enough support. Charlie grabbed Daniel's left hand and raised his arm so it was horizontal to the ground, and then he crouched and walked under it. When Charlie rose back up to his full height he completely bore the body weight of Daniel's left side. The twins would have to hike like Siamese twins joined at their side. Then there was Billy.

Billy kept trying to stop and lie down to take a little nap. Wendy would talk him out of it by getting him talking about cooking. Billy would then tell her detailed step-by-step procedures for cooking certain meals as they hiked.

Whenever he finished explaining a complete full course meal and preparations, he would stop and sit down and say, "Now I'm just going to take a little nap!" And so it went.

While Billy was describing what he would prepare if he was serving the President a five-course meal, Wendy's thoughts drifted to Adam. He said he *"Walks by faith, not by sight."* Now, Wendy was trusting that he would somehow be able to rescue her grandpa all by himself. She wondered why he would risk it?

He had faith that he could do it by himself. He definitely wasn't trusting in his sight. She was worried about his safety. In her mind she said, *God, I'm not sure if you're real or not because I can't see you. But Adam has faith in you. I guess I want you to protect him and help him rescue my grandpa. I'm putting my faith in him and that is making me walk by faith, not by sight. If my grandpa and Adam come home, I promise I will explore faith in you.*

Billy's voice became audible in her mind again, "And that's what I would serve the President! Now I'm going to lie down and take a little siesta."

In five hours, they came upon campsite #1 when Charlie stopped and said, "Look up."

Just above his head was a grenade trip line. They had left the grenade perimeter up when they left.

The drop site would be a half mile to their right. Instead of going to the cave, they could correct course and be at the drop site in forty-five minutes if they kept their same hiking speed—although it was not a pace that anyone would call speed. The sky had been light for an hour. A single shriek echoed up the mountains. Then multiple howls followed. They froze as the wave of fear released by the sound waves washed through them.

The adrenaline released by fear-driven shock seemed to flip a switch and sober up Billy out of his concussive stupor.

He yelled, "They are running up that mountain right now and cooks aren't food! We have to get to the cave!"

"What about the drop site?" asked Charlie.

Billy answered, "We don't have time to get to both the drop site and the cave. They are really close but we might have a chance to make it to one place. We can't defend the drop site! The cave will be our best chance to live!"

Not waiting for debate, Billy turned and started running down the mountain toward Nose Rock yelling, "Let's go!"

"And he's back, folks!" said Wendy.

"This is probably the first time in my life that Billy will beat me in a foot race," said Daniel.

"We'll see about that!" said Charlie as he leaned to his left, lifting Daniel completely off the ground, and started running downhill.

Wendy looked back in the direction they had come from and shivered. She wondered if she would ever see her grandpa again. She wondered if Billy, Charlie, and Daniel would ever see Adam again. Then she thought, *Watch, Crazy Joe will make it out of here and the rest of us won't.* She started running and yelled out loud as though Adam could hear her, "THIS IS THE WORST FIRST DATE IN THE WORLD!"

44

The Rescue

IN THE DANK DARKNESS of his subterranean crypt, Adam wondered if he would have enough air. In his mind he knew that the bushes and sticks covering the opening were not forming an air-tight seal, but claustrophobia seemed to be winning the battle over reason. Adam knew phobias were not always reasonable, like leporiphobia, the fear of rabbits. But then again, sometimes they could also keep people from harm like galeophobia, the fear of sharks.

Adam felt a cramp gripping his hamstring. He tried to adjust his body position, but there was no room and a clump of moist dirt fell on his head from the roots above him. He freaked out thinking it was a spider and smacked his face and rubbed his head. He needed to calm down and he knew it. He prayed.

He prayed for Daniel and his injury. Then for Charlie to have strength to carry his brother. And for Billy's mental faculties to return and the concussion to be gone. Then he thought of Wendy.

Adam was counting on her to help his brothers. And he saw the hope and desperation in her eyes when he said he would get Crazy Joe by himself. She was counting on him. Adam was used to his brothers counting on him, but knowing that Wendy was counting on him unlocked something deep inside that he had never expected. No woman had ever looked at him like she did. He realized she was putting all her faith in him.

The weight of life and death fell heavily on him. He had always felt responsible for his brothers and their welfare, but Wendy wasn't asking him to be responsible. She was trusting and believing that he would succeed. She was putting her faith in him. He wondered if this kind of faith was the same as that needed for a good marriage. Could a man and woman really trust and believe in each other and believe that their spouse would succeed in any quest on their behalf? He prayed for God to help him, and he prayed for Crazy Joe.

He lost track of time while he was praying, as though it had transported him to some spiritual realm separate from time. When he finished his prayers and opened his eyes, he saw the dark gray of early morning light poking through the bushes and branches concealing him.

Adam listened and thought he heard a faint noise in the still mountain air. It was a noise, but it wasn't in the air, it was in the earth. He could hear heavy footsteps and they were growing louder. The earth was transmitting a sound wave through the soil. A deep thud . . . he listened. Many thuds and they were close.

Adam was concerned that the pounding of his racing heartbeat would be audible. Then he worried about his breathing. Would they hear it? He tried to slow his breathing, but his heart seemed to have taken control of his respiratory system. Then the log shook above him. He felt a large thud on the ground and it vibrated through him. The creatures were standing around the log.

The solid steel of the Glock 19 in his hand didn't stop the fearful tremble rippling through Adam's fingers. Deep raspy wheezing and gurgling sounds bubbled through the air. Adam heard an exchange of low, mumbling chatter and then a forceful grunt, followed by the sound of dissipating footsteps moving down the mountain following the exact path Wendy, Charlie, Daniel, and Billy traversed. He waited until he heard silence. Then he waited another ten minutes before plowing out of his den.

Adam hefted his pack and rifle and went to retrieve the tripwire grenades from the perimeter. Adam collected the grenades carefully and began his ascent to the ridge of the mountain. He planned to walk the ridge line over to the next range, which started off with the flat-topped mountain where the drone was assaulted while hovering over Crazy Joe's makeshift flag.

It took him two hours to make it to the edge of the large meadow. He stayed in the tree line and quietly worked his way around the meadow toward the area where they had murdered the drone. He reached the base of a big tree, with no sign of any bigfoot. He looked around the tree to see an open area and the thirty-foot face of the granite rock face with the crevice.

Sitting on the ground to the left of the crack was the Boss. It had been a year since Adam had seen him but he looked the same. The Boss looked very similar to a silverback gorilla basking in the sun at any zoo in the world, only much larger and not contained in an enclosure to keep spectators safe.

Adam trembled. He didn't feel safe. His heart raced as he quietly took off his pack, concealed from the Boss by the large tree base. He carefully raised his rifle, a Remington 700 with a scope.

High above him in the tree, a furry, black head with a reddish-orange stripe poked out from the thick branch when it heard the metallic click of Adam chambering a round. As Adam took a knee to shoot from the kneeling position and raised the scope to his eye, the Cup Thief threw the broken drone. It hit the rifle, startling Adam and jolting his tense reflexes. A shot rang out, hitting the rock face just left of the Boss's head. Adam looked up to see the

Cup Thief flipping his lip back and shaking his head up and down.

The Boss roared and Adam dropped his rifle as the sound wave shook his entrails. He reached for his backpack, realizing he only had seconds before the Boss would be on him. He grabbed a grenade, pulled the pin and reached around the tree, dropping it on the other side. Adam fell to the ground behind the big tree, pulling his rifle close to his body and covering his ears. The Boss was coming.

The grenade exploded right as the Boss jumped toward the tree. He was airborne fifteen feet away from the tree when the explosive's concussive wave reversed his flight path and filled him with shrapnel. The Boss landed on his back on the ground twenty-two feet away, unconscious.

A popping sound started coming from the base of the tree, and the tree leaned. Adam got up from the ground on the other side of the tree, double checked his chambered round in the rifle and looked around the base of the tree. He saw the motionless body of the Boss, and then quickly aimed his rifle up to the branch above him searching for the Cup Thief. The Cup Thief had frantically climbed to the top of the tree after the explosion and was out of sight.

From the dark rock crevice thirty yards away, a voice cried out, "Is it safe?"

Adam yelled, "I think so."

Two pale figures cautiously poked their heads out and looked around and then slowly emerged from the narrow crack.

Adam ran over to them; surprised, he yelled out, "Eric!"

"I can't believe you are here!" said Eric, hugging Adam tight.

"You can thank Crazy Joe for that!" said Adam.

"Guys, we gotta move now before that red banshee comes back!" said Crazy Joe.

A loud crack and popping sound made them all jump and look toward the big tree. Adam could now see that the explosion eviscerated more than half of the tree's base. The tree moaned and leaned towards them slowly, and then it just kept coming. More pops and cracks from the base, as the top of the gigantic tree picked up speed on its downward ascent. Adam yelled, "Run!"

45

Run For Your Life!

THEY RAN INTO THE clearing by Nose Rock, with the bigfoot close on their heels. Charlie and Daniel arrived at the cave first, with Billy right behind them. Charlie climbed up the rope into the cave and prepared to pull up Daniel. But Daniel made it up by climbing the rope without even using his legs at all.

"Well, alrighty then!" said Charlie with surprise.

"Don't worry, you can pull up Billy!" said Daniel.

Billy was struggling as expected and Charlie pulled him up the last one-third of the way. They heard the mountain erupt with screams and roars.

Wendy broke into the opening wide-eyed, running as fast as she could. Seconds later the trees behind her moved as her pursuers shot into the opening, screaming and howling. They galloped out on all fours, side by side, and screaming.

Daniel yelled, "Guns!"

By the time they got their guns and looked back, there were three bigfoots twenty yards to Wendy's right and almost parallel to her. Another two were just fifteen yards to her left side but not quite parallel. The boys opened fire.

The three on Wendy's right accelerated when the volley of bullets started. One fell to the ground dead, shot through the eye. The other two kept running and arced to close the distance of separation and cut in front of Wendy to cut her off from reaching the cave. The two on the left side of Wendy had accelerated and were completely parallel to Wendy.

A bullet ripped into the knee of one and it went down hard. The other one pulled up and stopped and went back to help the wounded. Charlie saw that there were no bigfoots flanking Wendy's left side, but that there were about to be two bigfoots in between the cave and Wendy placing her directly in the line of fire.

He yelled, "We are about to lose her! Keep shooting!" and he jumped out of the cave.

Charlie hit the ground and rolled smoothly, transitioning right into a full run.

He ran a slant pattern to his right, yelling, "Wendy, run to me!" She changed her direction, running toward her left and towards Charlie. The bigfoot closest to Wendy went down hard as a bullet pierced into its ear, sloshing its brain. Charlie stopped running and pulled a grenade from his pocket, pulled the pin and dropped it at his feet right before Wendy made it to him.

Afraid she would stop, he yelled run and pointed and turned to follow behind her, placing his body between her and the lone pursuer. Charlie took three full strides and dove forward, pushing Wendy to the ground and landing on top of her. The grenade exploded, sending the pursuing bigfoot's body flying. Surprisingly, the injured beast got up screaming and ran toward the forest.

Billy came running up to Charlie and pulled him off of Wendy and onto his feet. He then reached into his pocket and pulled out another grenade, handing it to Charlie. Billy helped Wendy up to her feet and handed her a grenade. And then Billy grabbed a Glock from his belt. They saw three bigfoots retreating.

One was carrying an injured brown bigfoot over its shoulder like a fireman's carry. The other one was walking but in obvious pain from being turned into a shrapnel pincushion. The shrapnel from the grenade had ended the chase.

When they made it to the tree line, the one filled with shrapnel stopped and turned around and let out a thirty-second roar.

Billy yelled, "Oh, shut up!" and grabbed another grenade from his pocket, pulled the pin and threw it as far as he could toward the bigfoot.

Wendy pulled the pin from the grenade in her hand and threw it yelling, "You made me run; I hate running!"

Inspired, Charlie pulled the pin on his grenade and threw it yelling, "I got shrapnel in my butt!"

The three successive explosions made the bigfoots roar sound like a little mouse squeak. The bigfoots disappeared into the forest.

Billy said, "Let's get back in the cave."

46

On The Move!

Adam, Eric, and Crazy Joe ran towards the meadow. High-pitched squealing came from the fallen tree behind them. When they were crossing through the meadow, they saw the Red Zombie entering the far edge of the meadow with a wriggling raccoon in her hands. She looked at them and screamed, throwing the writhing raccoon back toward the forest.

She took a step toward them when another high-pitched squeal came from the fallen tree forty yards behind them. She stopped. Her narrowed eyes widened, and she dropped to all fours and galloped wide to the right, circling around them toward the big fallen tree. Adam raised his rifle, but she was moving too fast for him to scope her.

He said, "Let's keep going!"

By the time they made it to the far edge of the meadow and started up the mountain, the high-pitched squealing had stopped.

Behind them the Red Zombie was at the side of the Cup Thief. He was squealing and lying on the ground with a leg pinned by a limb of the fallen tree. She grabbed the thick branch and pulled up and twisted using the powerful force of her grip and muscular arms to shred the dense wood's strong fibers, breaking the branch where it connected to the trunk. The Cup Thief wiggled free and hobbled along the ground whimpering with one foot dragging.

The Cup Thief led her through the debris to the Boss. She found him lying unconscious next to the tree with shards of the grenade splintered throughout his torso. She slapped him and his eyes fluttered. She raised her hand to slap him again. His eyes flashed open and he grabbed her hand before it made contact again and growled at her showing his teeth.

The Boss sat up and blinked. He shook his head several times and coughed. He stood up and climbed over the fallen tree. Walking over to the rock crevice, he peered inside to confirm the vacancy. He walked around the granite rock face and climbed up the sloping backside to the peak. Once on top, he let out a booming forty-five-second roaring howl and then waited fifteen seconds for the echo to bounce off the surrounding mountain peaks before he did it again. He did this ten times. The Cup Thief watched.

Far away on another mountain peak, an old mangy, hunched-back beast rose to his feet. His splotchy gray hair glistened in the sun. He lifted his mostly bald head, pointing his wrinkly spotted face to the sky and let out a forty-second howl that started with a low pitch, then raised to a high pitch and then dropped low again. He did this ten times. When he finished, coyote packs all over the mountains responded.

The old gray hunchback moved quickly toward the Boss. As he traveled, red-haired soldiers appeared, running in the forest around him. Whooping and hooting filled the forest. The red army was on the move. The Boss waited.

The eerie calls echoing through the mountains made Adam, Crazy Joe, and Eric climb up the mountain faster.

"I may be free but I don't feel safe!" said Eric.

"There's a war coming, boys!" warned Crazy Joe.

"Hopefully, we can get out of here before that happens!" said Adam.

"Expect and prepare for the worst!" said Crazy Joe.

Adam looked back at Crazy Joe and said, "We have more weapons if we can make it to them!"

"Go faster!" said Eric with trembling voice.

Adam took his walkie-talkie out of his pack and powered it up; tuning it to Channel 5, he pressed the button and said, "Bigfoot Brothers over?" . . . Nothing. "Bigfoot Brothers, come in?" . . . Nothing. Adam wondered if they were still alive.

"Did everybody come?" asked Eric.

"Yes!" confirmed Adam.

"Where are they?" asked Eric.

"We got attacked and Daniel and Billy got hurt and Charlie and Wendy had to help them get back to the cave," replied Adam.

Crazy Joe shouted, "WENDY? You brought Wendy up here?"

"I couldn't stop her!" said Adam.

Crazy Joe grinned and said, "She's crazy!"

"I wonder where she gets that from?" said Adam.

Crazy Joe puffed out his chest and said, "I have no idea!"

The walkie talkie crackled to life, "Hey Adam, are you out there?"

Adam replied, "Yeah, Charlie, I'm here and I got Eric and Crazy Joe with me."

"We are at the cave; we just went head-to-head with five Bigfoots! We killed two of them and injured one," reported Charlie.

Adam asked, "Did any of you get hurt?"

Billy piped in from his walkie talkie, "Charlie's butt cheeks got some grenade fragments in them. Wendy is doctoring him up."

Eric laughed. Crazy Joe motioned to Adam for a turn on the walkie talkie. Adam handed it over to Crazy Joe.

"Hey, Wendy! Who is crazy now?" asked Crazy Joe.

Wendy's voice crackled back, "You are in so much trouble, old man!"

Taking back the walkie talkie, Adam asked, "How is Daniel?"

Daniel came on his walkie talkie and said, "I'll live. It hurts bad, but it isn't infected. How is Eric?"

Eric's squeaky voice transmitted back, "Skinnier and hungry."

Billy picked up his walkie talkie and said, "You are always hungry! I will cook you whatever you want when we get out of here! Where are you guys right now?"

Adam took the walkie talkie from Eric and said, "We should be at campsite #1 in about an hour if we don't have any trouble."

A voice buzzed back, "Hey, Adam, this is Charlie; we thought we heard some howls about a half hour ago—did you hear anything?"

Adam said, "Yeah, that was right after our escape! We were close to them, and we heard an answer come from a mountain far away."

Crazy Joe looked at Adam and reminded him, "They were calling in reinforcements! We need to hurry! They will be here soon!" and started running.

Adam picked up the pace and asked Charlie, "Did you guys get the second supply drop?"

Charlie buzzed back, "No!"

"Okay, we are going there before we come to you. We will radio you after we get the weapons—over and out," said Adam.

"Hurry up! . . . And keep an eye out for the three we ran off; they might be coming right towards you. One is shot in the leg and being carried," warned Charlie.

"Roger that!" answered Adam.

Eric asked for the walkie talkie. Adam handed it back to him as they ran.

Eric pressed the button and said, "Billy, I want a huge cake when we get home! Over?"

"You got it, little buddy!" replied Billy.

Eric smiled and started thinking about cake flavors as he ran . . . but in his excitement, he forgot to turn off the walkie talkie.

Adam yelled, "Stop!"

Crazy Joe kept running and blurted out, "We don't have time!"

"Do you want a weapon?" asked Adam.

Joe stopped abruptly and quickly turned around and said, "What do you got?"

"I have a Glock, this rifle, or hand grenades," said Adam.

Crazy Joe said, "Give me the Glock and a grenade."

Adam handed them over and looked at Eric. Eric was standing there wheezing and looking pale.

Eric wheezed, "Give me the rifle."

"No way! Don't you remember this whole thing started with you and a gun?" said Adam.

Adam reached in his pack and pulled out a granola bar and a grenade and handed them to Eric and said, "Listen! You pull the pin and you throw it immediately! Got it?

Eric nodded.

"Let's go!" said Adam as he started running to catch up to Crazy Joe.

THE CUP THIEF HAD two tight fists of red back hair. The Red Zombie stopped and flared her nostrils, testing the air. The scent of their escaped captive wasn't hard to find. She was getting close. Behind her, the Boss and the gray hunchback followed with thirty red warriors. While waiting for the red army, the Boss had dug out thirteen pieces of grenade fragments embedded in his body. With each bloody piece, his resolve to bring an end to these hairless invaders deepened.

The Red Zombie stopped and spread her arms out birdlike. Behind her, the red army spread out to her left and right. She lifted her hands, palms up toward the sky, and then turned them down to face the ground. The army dropped to all fours. She then flicked her fingers a few times, and the army surged forward quickly and silently into the dense brush. The Boss and the gray hunchback stayed back and waited.

Just then, three bigfoots came walking over the ridge. One was carrying another bigfoot over its shoulder. When they saw the Boss, the leader let out a loud whoop. The Boss pivoted quickly and gave an angry glare and emitted a low reverberating growl from deep within his chest.

Nearby, in a small meadow, human voices screamed. The Boss, the Cup Thief, the Red Zombie and the gray hunchback each climbed tall trees to enjoy the massacre.

47

Whack A Mole!

CRAZY JOE HEARD THE whoop and looked up just in time to see a blur of red fur flash between some trees.

He screamed, "They're here!" and pointed his Glock toward the tree line.

Adam dropped the yellow bag he had just picked up and turned with his rifle raised and ready. Eric gripped his grenade tighter. Adam fired a shot in the direction he saw Crazy Joe pointing the Glock, thinking it might scare them away. Nothing moved.

Feeling exposed, Eric screamed, "I don't want to be here!"

"Let's get to the cave!" said Adam as he took the walkie talkie from Eric, tried to power it up. It was dead. He yelled, "That's just great!" and threw it.

Adam picked up the yellow bag with his left hand and brandished the rifle with his right hand. When he turned to begin the trek toward the cave, he saw a massive red beast's torso lean out to peek around a big tree. Then he saw another one peeking from behind another tree ten yards to its right. And then another.

"We are totally surrounded!" said Eric.

"If they all come at us at once, we are dead!" said Crazy Joe. Adam dropped the yellow bag and opened it up and dumped the contents out. fifteen grenades rolled on the ground, a shotgun and two boxes of shells, another Glock, and four extra clips.

"Everyone, get a grenade and let's get back to back," said Adam.

A loud roar seemed to come from the sky, and a high-pitched roar joined in. All around them, the forest erupted with roars. Eric put down his grenade and covered his ears and crouched down into the fetal position, crying. Then a loud piercing shriek penetrated the air and the red army charged.

Adam pulled the pin, tossed his grenade and reached for another. Crazy Joe tossed his grenade and looked over at Eric still on the ground and pulled out his Glock and fired five shots at two beasts nearly on top of them as the grenades went off. They fell eight feet away.

"Get up, Eric, or we're all dead!" yelled Adam.

Eric screamed, stood up and pulled the pin on his grenade and threw it. It landed and then exploded in the hand of a lanky orangish-red beast that had tried to pick it up to throw it back.

"Reload!" screamed Adam.

Eric picked up the shotgun. Adam and Crazy Joe grabbed more grenades. By the time they looked up again, there were multiple attackers coming. Some on all fours and some running on two legs. Eric started blasting the shotgun. Grenades were thrown and Glocks emptied. When a beast fell, another seemed to appear in its place instantaneously. After twenty minutes things went quiet. The meadow was littered with thirteen hairy corpses.

For the next thirty minutes, everything was quiet. Adam thought they might have given up, but then he saw something move high above in the trees. He took inventory. They had five grenades left, one box of shotgun shells, eleven bullets left for the rifle, and two magazines for the Glocks.

If the red army attacked a few more times, they would run out of ammo. They needed to conserve bullets and grenades. Adam didn't know how many bigfoots there were, but since they stopped coming, he figured they had convinced them to stop charging.

"They will not stop coming until we are all dead or they are," said Crazy Joe.

"How do you know that?" asked Adam.

Crazy Joe pulled out a hanky, blew his nose, and said, "Commandment #3: 'What I know.' I know for a fact that these creatures have a strong sense of justice. If you injure them, they will injure you or make you suffer. That's how I knew Eric was still alive.

He injured one of them, and so they took him for payback . . . except they like payback to last a long time. It's their weakness. If you kill one of them, then they will fight to the death to kill you no matter how unevenly matched . . . another weakness. So, believe me, they will keep coming."

"We could try to make a run for the cave?" said Adam.

"The minute we got in the forest they would get close to us and grab us before we could even see them. There is too much cover for them and we're too slow. This is the best place for a standoff!" said Crazy Joe.

"Until it gets dark," said Eric.

"That's probably what they are waiting for since they have seen our firepower," said Adam.

In the forest, a tree fell. Then another. Then another. Trees were being pushed down on every side of them. For the next three hours, they kept hearing and sometimes seeing the crashing of trees. Then rocks the size of baseballs were launched at them. Whenever the rocks were launched, they would come as a steady hail.

While Adam, Crazy Joe, and Eric were busy ducking out of the way of rock missiles, a tree would be thrown and flipped end over end into the meadow. After an hour, Adam realized what they were doing. They were literally moving the forest closer.

They were hiding behind the fallen trees, then pushing another fallen tree up to the last fallen tree, and whenever the rock attack happened, they would stand up the tree on end, and throw it or flip it forward closer to the three objects of their wrath. The creatures could then belly crawl up behind these trees without detection, and repeat the process.

If the beasts kept this up, in a few hours they would be close enough to swarm and attack from every direction with speed and overwhelming numbers, rendering defense weapons useless.

"We can't let them keep their construction project going! They are essentially building barricades to get closer to us. We have got to pick them off!" said Adam.

"How?" asked Eric.

Adam looked at him and smiled.

"Why are you smiling? I don't like it when you smile at me! . . . What?" asked Eric.

"You are the bait, Me and Crazy Joe are the snipers!" explained Adam.

"Really?" asked Eric.

Adam and Crazy Joe just smiled.

Eric would run about twenty yards away from Adam and Crazy Joe like he was going to run into the forest. Then bigfoot heads would pop up in the bushes and peek around trees. Then WACK! A sniper shot would take care of business if the shot was good.

"I love playing Whac A Mole!" yelled Crazy Joe.

Whenever Eric would run back to Adam and Crazy Joe, more rocks would rain down and trees would be rolled, flipped or thrown closer. Then, as soon as he could, Eric would go again. Each time he got bolder.

Eric began trash talking, "You smell like your breath—butt breath!"

One time, he even pulled down his pants and smacked his butt at them and said, "You smell like this!" . . . Thwack! . . . A rock hit him in the left cheek. After that, rocks started flying at him whenever he popped out and ran.

It had turned into a sick game of dodgeball. Eric would dodge rocks and bigfoot would try to dodge bullets. Eric got hit multiple times, but no bones were broken. He began picking up small sticks and branches from the ground when he could and brought them back to the base.

In five hours of battle, Adam sniped six bigfoots and Crazy Joe shot three. Even with all those casualties, it didn't stop the shrinking of the meadow. The meadow had gradually shrunk to the point that there were tree barricades all around them. They had only a twenty-yard buffer.

High in the trees the Red Zombie let out a piercing screech. The gray hunchback let out a piercing howl and coyotes all over the mountains went berserk. The Boss followed suit and let out a deep, long, mournful wail. On a large limb near the Boss, the

Cup Thief snapped a branch and threw it, letting out his best pre-pubescent roar. Then the rest of the red army roared, and they began moving into positions, belly crawling from fallen tree to fallen tree, creeping closer to their prey. It was dusk. It wouldn't be long now.

48

The Final Attack!

ADAM WAS DISCUSSING A plan to cause a distraction and make a break for the cave when the attack came.

Crazy Joe interrupted Adam yelling, "Wake up, boys, it's time to make jerky!"

He pulled the pin on a grenade, and threw it in front of three giants galloping on all fours side by side, shrinking the twenty yards rapidly with each lope. Their snarling stopped when the blast sent their mangled bodies flying. Adam and Eric each pulled pins and threw grenades towards advancing death squads. Everything went eerily quiet.

Eric broke the silence, "Is that all of them?"

Then trees came flying from each side, landing within ten feet of them.

"That first wave was a test to see what we would do. This time they will keep coming until they get us. Let's let them get really close before we drop the grenades and maybe we can kill more of them that way," said Crazy Joe.

"Okay, not until we see the demons in their eyes!" yelled Adam.

"I'm going to close my eyes and throw!" said Eric.

"Don't!" Shouted Crazy Joe and Adam in unison.

Eric had dragged back enough sticks during the sniper-dodge rock game that they could have a small fire. Adam lit the fire and they stood around it with their backs to it, forming a triangle, with grenades and guns at their feet. Shrieks echoed once again from the treetops, and then the ground shook.

Adam yelled, "Here they come!"

Behind the fallen trees all around the meadow, hairy red and brown warriors slapped the ground with open hands. Then there was another shriek from the treetops, and all the beasts began slapping their chests. The resulting popping sound was louder than the sound of a hundred wooden baseball bats hitting trees with great force. The sounds went from thuds to thunderous banging. Then a loud roar came from the treetops and the army all roared at the same time and charged.

Crazy Joe yelled, "I change my mind! Don't let them get close! We need time to reload!" and threw his grenade.

A fast, brown giant jumped from the ground onto the fallen tree thirty feet away and took one enormous leap toward Eric, landing just ten feet in front of him. It took one step and leaped again. Eric ducked to pick up his last grenade right as the flying body was about to tackle him. It missed and landed right in the fire. Adam turned and shot it in the head.

Crazy Joe threw his last grenade and yelled, "Time for guns!"

The number of bodies coming toward them had slowed down to the point that there were ten to thirty seconds between them. Adam knew they would be out of ammunition in a few minutes.

"I need a weapon!" yelled Eric, fully panicked.

"Lay on the ground and play dead!" answered Adam.

Eric went to lie down and saw the half-burnt bigfoot corpse. He grabbed two fistfuls of shaggy back-hair and laid on the body and rolled. He ended up under the body, his skinny frame totally covered by the malodorous smoldering cadaver.

Click-Click-Click! Crazy Joe threw the Glock, and pulled out a buck knife yelling, "Time to slice and dice!" Adam's rifle clicked and he swung the butt of the rifle in a violent arc crushing the skull of a red female beast.

Crazy Joe jumped on top of her as she fell to the ground and stabbed her ten times singing, "Cuts to the heart and you're to blame, baby—you give love a bad name!"

His blade hit a bone and broke.

Adam screamed, "Kick the fire and spread it out so we can see better!"

A hunchback silhouette stood and looked down from atop the high end of a log twenty feet away that had one end of the log sitting on top of another log creating the high point. Unaware of the hunched figure, Crazy Joe kicked the fire and burning branches flew toward the tree. The flicker of light lit up a snarling, bald-spotted face.

Crazy Joe made eye contact with the beast. He recognized the creature as the leader of the troop he had battled against so many years before when he was a kid. The hunched beast's eyes flashed as he recognized Joe. He grimaced as he began running down the log toward Crazy Joe with his eyes thirsty for bloody revenge.

Crazy Joe's hand shot into his pocket and pulled out a small spray bottle, pointed it, and sprayed the beast's face when it was eight feet away. It screamed in pain and stopped. Rubbing its face and emitting inhumane screams, it reached for the ground and grabbed fistfuls of dirt and rubbed dirt on its eyes and face and crammed dirt into its nostrils.

Then it looked at Crazy Joe and Adam, raised its arms up slowly, and let out a low, slobbery, vibrating growl. Six bigfoot heads popped up from the logs behind him and then the creatures rose to their full heights, all nine feet in stature. In unison, the death squad all stepped over the log and marched up beside the bald hunchback.

Adam and Crazy Joe took a step back, and both tripped over the carcass Eric was hiding under. Eric raised his head up a little and peeked out, seeing the seven creatures looking at him.

"Oh, crap!" he said and ducked back under the carcass. The bald hunchback screamed and leaped to kill.

From behind Adam and Crazy Joe came a loud hissing sound, followed immediately by a loud whoosh and a hot ball of flames. The fire stream shot over their heads and hit the hunchback right in the chest right as the bald hunchback leaped on top of Crazy Joe sinking a yellow canine tooth deep into his shoulder.

The tooth clicked and popped as it broke out of the withered gum-line of the geriatric attacker. It had hit Joe's collarbone. Adam rolled over and stabbed out his arm sharply, sinking the blade of his Swiss Army knife into the temple of the old hairy ape man, rendering it instantly into a lifeless, smoldering hominid.

The stream of flames swooped from side to side, soaking the wall of the creatures in oil-soaked flames. They each fell to the ground screaming and rolling, but the stream of flames kept spraying them like a garden of death was being watered with hellfire. When the charcoaled bodies all stopped moving, the flames stopped shooting.

"You guys want to stop playing around and get out of here now?" shouted Wendy.

"Absolutely!" said Adam and Crazy Joe as they scrambled to get up. The hairy carcass on the ground next to them started to move and Wendy aimed the flame thrower at it and Adam yelled "NO!" and pushed the nozzle up into the air just in time, causing the twenty-foot flame to spray straight up in the air.

Eric emerged from under his hairy cadaver cocoon, gawking at the flame. Wendy took her finger off the trigger and said, "Oh, hi!"

Eric's eyes bulged, and he said, "You're hot!"

They all laughed. Crazy Joe stumbled toward Wendy, "Can we go home now? I think I need a donut!" and he fainted.

49

Reunited

Wendy revived her grandpa and then pulled a granola bar from her pocket and made him eat it. Crazy Joe rode on Adam's back like a wrinkled, hundred-pound backpack on the trip down the mountainside to Nose Rock and the cave. The Boss looked down over the meadow from the top of a giant sequoia. His brow furrowed as he scanned the flame-lit bodies scattered throughout the meadow.

He had seen the gray hunchback burn with his death squad. The gray hunchback should've stayed in the position of high command with the Boss, the Red Zombie, and the Cup Thief rather than enter the fray. But there was a story in his eyes that the Boss read. It was the story of a long overdue vengeance for spilled blood, death, and undoubtedly, his flame-scarred-head and spotted face, but now his story had ended.

Billy was boiling beans in the cave when Wendy's voice echoed through the dark, "Can you send down the elevator, please?" Three heads looked over the edge.

"Coming down!" yelled Charlie as he grabbed the rope and jumped over the edge in one motion, repelling off the rock face with one push.

"Ladies first," said Charlie extending the rope to Wendy.

Wendy glared at him and then smiled and said, "Wrong! Old men and POW survivors first!"

"Yeah! Don't you recognize me, Charlie?" said Eric.

Charlie looked at Eric and said, "You're so skinny! You were two percent milk before, now you're non-fat!"

"You know I'm lactose intolerant, right?" said Eric laughing.

Eric tried to climb up the rope into the cave but was too weak, so Charlie tied the rope around his chest and Billy pulled him up.

Then Adam climbed up with Crazy Joe on his back singing, "Oh I'll fly away—Oh Lordy, I'll fly away!"

Wendy tied the flame thrower to the rope sending it up before her. She had impatiently free-climbed halfway up the rock face before they dropped the rope down for her.

After they were all in the cave sitting around a fire, Daniel asked, "Eric, how in the heck are you alive? We all saw your bones and your bloody t-shirt in a grave!"

Eric cocked his head to the left as his mind replayed his capture, "They were eating a dead deer behind that big rock when I ran up. They grabbed me and pounded me with their open hands and scratched the heck out of me, shredding my t-shirt. I was in so much shock I couldn't even scream . . . then I fainted. One of them carried me off. I guess they must've shown you the deer's bones . . . So, that's why you didn't come sooner? You thought I was dead?"

"Yep!" said Adam. "Thank God for Crazy Joe or you would have spent the rest of your life there!"

"I would have gone crazy!" said Eric.

Crazy Joe interjected, "That's why Crazy Joe had to come and get you! We can't have too many crazy people in this world."

"Thanks, Crazy Joe!" said Eric. Then looking at Billy he said, "Can I have some beans now?"

Adam pulled a GPS transmitter out of the corner of the cave that he had left behind a rock and turned it on to signal the helicopter pilot. Billy sloshed some beans into a zip lock baggy and handed it to Eric. Eric took them and bowed his head and prayed the Lord's prayer really fast. When he finished, he looked up and saw everyone wiping their eyes.

He chuckled and said, "If you are crying now, just wait until these beans kick in!"

50

Airborne!

THE EARLY MORNING SKY lightened and hues of orange and gold danced on sun rays poking through the forest like little comet tails. Adam didn't feel the Boss, Red Zombie, and Cup Thief's eyes burning holes into him. They were peering out from behind large trees just four to five trees deep in the shadows of the tree-line. Adam's eyes were too busy searching the sky for the helicopter.

Adam kept checking the GPS transmitter to make sure it was still working. The blinking red LED light seemed to have the same urgency that had kept him awake all night. Everyone was together and safe, but Adam couldn't rest until he got everyone home. Only then would the saga that began more than a year ago with a hike to search for perspective and gold be over. Their lives had changed forever. They had faced great adversity and so many obstacles and had come out as more than conquerors.

The vwop-vwop-vwop-vwop of helicopter blades broke the morning silence.

Adam yelled, "Billy, Charlie, Daniel, Eric, Crazy Joe, Wendy, wake up! Let's go home!"

Each slumbering body in the cave quickly seemed to rise from the dead with the call of their name. By the time they were out of the cave with all the guns and gear, the helicopter had landed across the meadow on the other side of the rock. After they loaded up all the gear, Billy climbed in and turned to help Daniel in, followed by Eric and Charlie. The pilot had started up the blades when he saw the motley crew appear from around the rock. His eyes watched from behind his mirrored glasses.

He carefully watched them load the chopper, running mathematical calculations in his head.

He yelled over the whining roar of the blades, "No more!"

"What are you talking about?" yelled Adam.

The pilot shouted, "Too much weight! I'll come back for you!"

The pilot turned back to look at his control panel to flip a switch, when his eyes caught a huge rock crashing into his windshield. The glass cracked in a spiderweb pattern the size of a soccer ball directly in front of him. The glass had saved his chest from being shattered by the boulder's blunt force. The Red Zombie was standing in front of the copter with another large rock in her hands raised over her head.

The pilot pulled back on the stick right as she launched the granite cannonball toward his face. The nose of the chopper lifted, and the boulder hit underneath the nose of the copter. The pilot lifted the chopper off the ground and then flicked his joystick forward like he was tapping something one time with a hammer. The chopper lurched forward thirty feet with the nose dipped down and the tail raised. The Red Zombie turned to run, but the whirling blades splattered her torso into an exploding cloud of red mist. The pilot lifted the chopper above the tree line and banked the joystick to circle the meadow.

A loud, vicious roar from the sky drowned out the helicopter's dinning whine. Adam, Crazy Joe and Wendy looked up from their prostrate positions on the ground to see the Boss standing atop Nose Rock, looking down at them.

"Airborne!" screamed Crazy Joe, as he turned to run through the woods toward the high cliff above the river.

"Run, Wendy!" yelled Adam as he yanked on her arm to force her body to move out of the fear trance that had constricted her!

Wendy broke into a dead run, following her grandpa. Adam let go of her arm and ran behind her to place himself between her and the Boss.

The hulking Boss let out another blasting roar as he leapt from Nose Rock, landing on the ground with an earthshaking thud. In a split second, a silver and black blur shot past all three sprinting humans, barreling right through small trees, snapping them off like a bulldozer. Crazy Joe was only seven yards away from accomplishing his plan to cliff dive to freedom when the Boss appeared in his path. Crazy Joe came to a stop only five yards away. Wendy and Adam pulled up, stopping next to Crazy Joe.

Another deafening roar assaulted them, and this time they felt the heat blast from the hot, rancid breath. Slobber strings dripped from its canines.

"Get behind me!" yelled Adam.

Crazy Joe looked at him and said, "Airborne always wins!" Crazy Joe ran right toward the Boss and tried to ankle tackle him by diving and wrapping his arms around his ankles and driving all of his weight into the hairy legs. The Boss didn't move a millimeter. It looked like Crazy Joe had run into a brick wall. He was still grunting, pushing and wincing, trying to exert force from every molecule of his scrawny one-hundred-pound body to push the Boss over the cliff.

The Boss raised his massive clenched fists above his head to smash down his arms like giant hammers and snap Crazy Joe's back like a twig. Adam took two steps and drove off of his legs to launch his body like a linebacker through the air and driving his shoulder right into the ribcage of the Boss. The Boss' weight shifted backwards just a little and his left foot moved back a step to help him stabilize.

Thrown off by the slight instability of his shifting weight, his muscular arms came down on Adam's shoulder blades at different speeds affecting the intended blunt force, dialing it down from bone breaking to terribly painful. Adam winced in pain. The Boss's left heel was on the very edge of the cliff and he gripped the ground with his toes and leaned his upper torso forward slightly.

Adam was pushing with all of his might and driving his legs like he was trying to push the back of a car that was out of gas. Crazy Joe was still straining away to keep his skinny arms wrapped around the thick hairy ankles in a tight grip. He had interlaced his fingers to help keep himself glued to the Boss's feet. Crazy Joe was now lying completely flat on the ground. His breathing had turned to weird, wheezing sounds now.

Wendy looked on in horror and realized they would not move the one-thousand-pound beast. In a flash, she pictured what was sure to happen next. It would kill them. First Adam, probably with the next crushing fist blows rained down onto his back or head.

Next, Crazy Joe would be picked up and completely ripped apart piece by piece, head, arms, and legs removed from their torso. Then finally, the Boss would come for her. She didn't want to think about what might happen to her.

She heard her grandpa's whimpering voice weakly say, "Airborne!" and thought about that being the last thing she would ever hear him say. Wendy's eyes sparked.

Wendy ran toward the Boss and she stepped on her grandpa's butt with her right foot and then stepped up onto Adam's lower back with her left foot like climbing stairs, and sprang forward and up sticking her right arm out to her side as her body sailed past the Boss' torso.

She screamed, "Airborne!"

Wendy clothes-lined him, striking his nose and face with all of her bodyweight bottled up in her arm and all of her body's mass flying past the creature toward the open expanse of sky above the river.

The Boss's eyes widened in surprise as his head snapped up and back, followed by his torso gripped by Adam. Adam felt the torso move six inches toward the abyss and drove hard with his legs, driving his shoulder forward and through the bulk in front of him. The creature was going down like a tree. Feet rooted securely in place but body tipping, careening and falling. When the creature's mass fell backwards and he fell towards the river below, Adam was still holding on to the torso and Crazy Joe was still attached to the beast's feet like a failing parachute.

There were three sounds when they landed below. One was a loud crack, and the other was a splash, and the third was groaning. Crazy Joe was splashing in the water, but still hanging on to one large hairy foot that was dangling limply off the edge of a large granite boulder surrounded by swirling water.

Adam was lying on top of the lifeless corpse between him and the top of the rock. The hairy mattress had broken his fall some, but Adam was groaning, trying to catch the wind that had been knocked out of his lungs. His side was hurting, and he wondered if he had a broken rib and punctured lung.

He looked up to see the head of the Boss split open on the boulder like a cracked egg with the pulverized runny contents draining out. When the Boss fell backward, the heavier mass of his giant shoulders, chest and upper back caused his landing to be head first. Lucky for the airborne crew, and unfortunate for him, he landed on the rock rather than in the cool water.

Wendy's voice rang out from the riverbank, "Are you okay?"

Crazy Joe spit water and yelled, "Airborne wins!"

Adam gave a forced smile with a groan and a thumb's sideways, to indicate he was in some pain. Wendy rushed over to him and helped him sit up slowly, while Crazy Joe unclenched his tangled arthritic fingers and swam to the side and dragged himself out of the water onto the gravelly bank, his cargo pockets scooped up river bottom gravel like a dredge.

The helicopter swooped over the trees and came into a holding position twenty feet above the rushing river, like a giant dragonfly.

A loudspeaker squawked from the copter, "Float downstream and get out at Gold Digger Falls. I will unload some weight and come back for you there!"

Charlie slid open the side door of the copter and jumped out yelling, "Airborne!"

Daniel smiled and followed, making peace signs while screaming, "Airborne!"

Eric yelled, "We started this together and we will finish it together!" and pinched his nose and stepped out of the copter.

"You are all crazy!" said Billy, looking down from the door.

Everyone below started yelling, "Jump, Billy! Jump!" And then, "Chicken!" Which quickly morphed into a group chant, "Billy's a chicken! Billy's a chicken!"

Billy yelled back "Cooks ain't chickens! We cook chickens!" and he jumped out awkwardly, landing with a loud slapping belly flop in the center of the river.

From under the water Billy heard everyone groan, "Ooooh!" Billy smiled under the water and stayed face down and motionless to mess with them. They all swam to the middle of the river to check on Billy.

The helicopter veered away, following the snaking river's path. They all floated down the river. From the cliff high above, they heard a loud high-pitched, warbly roar which drew their eyes up to see the shrieking Cup Thief frantically shaking a tree. Branches were twisted and broken off and thrown over the cliff.

He was distressed and in hysterics, with no family to console him. He would grow and become massive and strong like the Boss and fierce like the Red Zombie. He would walk the forest alone now, but forever he would be filled to his core with an unsubsiding rage and bloodthirsty grudge against all human beings.

51

Vindication

THE HELICOPTER PILOT CALLED his wife on his flight back to town to arrange for her to meet him at the helipad with her car to get the bags of guns and the flamethrower. They were all from his personal collection. Adam had known him since childhood. Adam had paid him seven thousand dollars up front for the gun rentals and ammo and the planned helicopter drops. Adam had promised him five thousand more on the return trip.

The pilot's wife called the news station to say her husband was picking up the Bigfoot Brothers from the woods and Eric Grimes was alive and with them. Her next calls were to the police department, the district attorney, and Eric's dad.

An hour later when the helicopter returned to the launchpad, there were news cameras, newspaper reporters, police officers, Detective Stewart, the district attorney, as well as sixty people who heard the news on their police scanners . . . and Eric Grimes' drunk dad. When the blades stopped whirling, the crowd swarmed the chopper. The police had to push everyone back to make room for the passengers to climb out of the copter.

Eric was the last to get out and everyone cheered . . . everyone except Detective Stewart and Darren Grimes.

The district attorney turned to Darren Grimes and said, "I'm dropping this civil suit against the Bigfoot Brothers."

Darren Grimes's face turned bright red and he turned and stumbled toward Eric shouting at him, "You cost me a million dollars, stupid! I wish you were dead!" and swung his balled-up fist toward his son's head, like he had so many times before.

But this time, instead of taking it, Eric dodged the blow and dropped his dad with a sharp elbow to the jaw.

Darren crumbled to the ground, shaking his head and dripping blood from a deep gash.

He started screaming, "Arrest him! Arrest him! I want him arrested for assault!"

The police sergeant stepped forward and placed Darren in handcuffs saying, "Actually, Mr. Grimes, that is what is called self-defense. You, however, are under arrest for drunk and disorderly conduct in public and if your son wants to press charges for assault, we'll add that charge on, too!"

Darren Grimes looked down and mumbled, "He should be dead."

The news cameras had captured the entire scene and were still rolling when Detective Stewart asked Eric, "Were you beat up and kidnapped by the Bigfoot Brothers?"

Eric looked at him like he was as drunk as his dad, "These guys saved my life! I was kidnapped by bigfoot!"

Stewart snarled, "You expect us to believe a bigfoot kidnapped you and held you in the mountains for over a year?"

"Actually, it was a whole bunch of bigfoots and my friends were the only ones who had the guts to come and get me," replied Eric.

"This is all a colossal fraud! You all made this up to sell T-shirts!" accused Stewart.

Detective Stewart turned to the district attorney and asked, "Can we charge them?"

The district attorney laughed and said, "Give it a break, Stewart! The kid's alive!"

Wendy stepped up to Stewart and said, "You laughed at me when I told you my grandpa was alive in those mountains. You suck at your job! The Bigfoot Brothers helped me find my grandpa, who had gone into the woods to rescue Eric. We went and found my grandpa and Eric and we killed a bunch of bigfoots in the process because nobody in this town believed these great men were telling the truth.

"This town treated them like criminals without any proof! If anyone should get sued in a civil lawsuit, it should be you and the authorities, and the legal system in this town!"

The crowd applauded as Detective Stewart turned and stormed away, pushing through the crowd.

———◆———

THE NEXT MORNING THE Bigfoot Brothers, Eric, Wendy, and Crazy Joe were all picked up by police and brought to a special press conference at city hall. The Mayor of the City, surrounded by the city leaders and the district attorney, presented all seven of them with key-to-the-city awards. At the advice of the district attorney, each of them was handed a check for $50,000 dollars and a public apology and heartfelt gratitude.

Then the Mayor stunned everyone when he announced that the city council met last night and unanimously voted to change the name of the city to Bigfoot Springs. After the ceremony, the Bigfoot Brothers' attorney, G. Dane, approached the Bigfoot Brothers with reporter Robert Hawk at his side. The Great Dane walked up behind Adam and patted him on the back.

Adam's broken rib screamed in pain, and he ducked away, emitting a loud, "Stop! Stop! Stop!"

The Great Dane said, "Oh sorry." Without a pause or any real empathy, he continued excitedly, "I have something here that will make you feel better!"

"I doubt it!" winced Adam.

The Great Dane cleared his throat and said, "Gentlemen and Lady, here in my hand, I have a one-and-half-million-dollar contract from Robert Hawk's News Station and Media Group asking for an exclusive interview with each of you for a documentary film and exclusive book-publishing rights for your story."

The Bigfoot Brothers and Eric all looked at each other and then to Adam. Adam shrugged and gave a questioning look to Wendy, and then Wendy passed the look on to Crazy Joe.

Crazy Joe shouted "Heck yes, we'll take it on one condition."

Robert Hawk nervously asked, "And what condition is that?"

Crazy Joe stared at him a long time for dramatic effect with his most serious deadpan face and then said, "You buy us all the donuts we can eat at the donut shop right now, and we'll sign the papers!"

Robert Hawk smiled at first but then, wanting to play along, made a face like this was a deal-breaker and sighed a heavy sigh, shaking his head side to side and said, "Let me confer with my lawyer."

He and the Great Dane whispered back and forth a few seconds before he turned back to Crazy Joe and said, "Okay, it's a deal! But only if my lawyer and I get our donuts first?"

Crazy Joe spit on his bony hand and stuck it out. Robert Hawk looked at Joe's hand. Joe wiggled his fingers a little as if to say, "Come on."

Robert Hawk wrinkled his nose a little in disgust and pretended to spit in his palm and shook Crazy Joe's hand with a limp hand.

Charlie laughed at Robert Hawk's face and jumped next to Crazy Joe, spit on his hand and stuck it out, saying, "That deal is with all of us, so you have to shake each of our hands to seal that deal!"

Robert Hawk looked at the Great Dane and asked, "Is this really necessary?"

The Great Dane smiled, nodded, and said, "Absolutely!"

Everyone laughed and lined up. Each handshake seemed to sap the strength and droop the shoulders of Robert Hawk, who just moments before was standing tall, confident, and proud like a puffed-up rooster in a hen house. After watching Robert Hawk make it successfully all the way down the gauntlet of soggy hands, Crazy Joe started walking, leading the parade down the street toward the donut shop.

He yelled out, "Woo-hoo! Feed me or fight me, T.V. man!"

52

Gold Digger's Donuts And Dreams

THE CHIEF WAS BANGING on the side of the T.V. with his back to the door. The donut shop doors flung open, jiggling the three little bells hanging from a string on the door handle.

Khamla looked up from behind the counter and gasped, "Crazy Joe!"

A warbling shout rang out from the doorway, "Gold Diggers, sound off!"

A carton of chocolate milk dropped from the hand of the fat man at the corner table in the Hawaiian shirt, splashing all over the table when he quickly stood up and saluted, "Home Run Johnny here, coach, still swinging for the fence!"

Crazy Joe replied, "Johnny, you're in the batting cage!"

The Chief had stiffened up like a statue and reported, "Chief Gold Digger here, holding down the fort!"

Crazy Joe saluted back at Johnny to put him at ease, and shuffled over to the Chief, "No time for that fort business now—Crazy Joe wants to see the gold!"

Still standing at attention facing the T.V., the Chief said, "I gave it to Wendy for your funeral on the mountain!"

"I ain't dead yet! Chief, look, here's your tiny little nugget necklace back," said Crazy Joe.

Khamla laughed, "No, remember his nugget bigger than yours? That why he get free donut, not you!"

Handing the Chief his nugget necklace back, Crazy Joe said, "Khamla, I am so glad you said that! Take a look at this!"

He reached in his pocket and held up a gold nugget that was twice as big as the Chief's.

Crazy Joe explained, "When I tackled the bigfoot into the river my pants pockets got filled up with dirt and rocks from the river bottom. This is what I found in my pocket when I got home and did my laundry!"

Khamla scowled.

Crazy Joe commanded victoriously, "Bring me my FREE donut!"

The Chief smiled and bent down to get a close look at Crazy Joe's nugget and whistled. They walked over to the table where Johnny was wiping up the spilled milk and sat down.

Wendy had been holding the group back just inside the entrance to watch her grandpa have his moment with the Gold Diggers.

"Khamla, we are all getting lots of donuts, do you want some help?" asked Wendy.

Khamla smiled, "Okay, that good; you come here—spend lot of money!"

The group shuffled in and found seats.

Homerun Johnny handed Eric a jelly donut, and said, "Here, this will help with the bigfoot P.O.W. – P.T.S.D! It has helped me. I was kidnapped by them, too!"

Eric looked at him and said, "Thanks! Sit down."

At another table, the Great Dane started going over the contract line by line with Adam and Robert Hawk.

A few minutes later, Khamla and Wendy walked over to the corner table and placed a plate in front of Crazy Joe that had an elongated bear claw donut made to look like a bigfoot foot print.

Crazy Joe beamed, "It's a bigfoot donut!"

"I made special for you. Wendy call me last night!" said Khamla.

Crazy Joe, emotional, said, "Thanks, sweeties!"

"You welcome crazy old man! You no more bother me about bigfoot donut okay?" replied Khamla.

Khamla turned to the Chief, "You lazy! You no go on trip to mountain with crazy old man! Now, he get free donut and coffee all the time! Chief with small nugget, no more free! Now you pay!"

Crazy Joe stood up and clanged his spoon on his coffee cup to get everyone's attention, "When we were surrounded by bigfoots and out of ammunition, that nasty-scarred face, bald, bigfoot jumped on me and had me pinned down. It tried to give me a kill bite to my neck. I was milliseconds away from dying, when Adam stabbed it in the head with a Swiss Army knife."

In a trembling voice, "Thank you for that, Adam! . . . I want you to have this necklace. I made it with the bigfoot canine I dug out of my shoulder last night."

"Thank you!" said Adam as he took the gift from Crazy Joe.

Everyone with moist eyes, said, "No, thank you, Adam!" and applauded.

When they were all on their third donut, Adam looked at Wendy and asked, "Will you go on a second date with me!"

"Well, I don't know; the first date was really lame," replied Wendy.

All the brothers went, "Oooh!"

Unfazed, Adam smiled and said, "I know, I know, the first date was pretty lame! . . . . Looking at his brothers, he continued, "We never got to be alone!"

Wendy laughed.

"Well, we had to keep him from messing it up!" explained Charlie.

Adam looked back into Wendy's eyes confidently, "Don't worry, for our second date we will go somewhere we can be alone."

"You are pretty confident this second date is going to happen, aren't you?" said Wendy.

Adam smiled, "As you are aware, I walk by faith not by sight!" Reaching in his pocket and pulling out an envelope, he said, "I have purchased two airline tickets to a gold-panning camp in Alaska and I am hoping you will join me for our second date?"

Wendy looked at her grandpa and he gave her an approving wink. Wendy looked back into Adam's questioning eyes and asked, "When do we leave?"

"The dream begins tomorrow!" answered Adam.

———◆———

FOR WE WALK BY faith, not by sight - 2 Corinthians 5:7 (KJV)

Thank you so much for reading Bigfoot Brothers!
I appreciate you!
Please do me a huge favor and take a few seconds
to rate it and leave an honest review on the online
store or stores of your choice that carry my book.
I would love to hear from you!
Email me at: info@chrisbossy.com
If you have encountered bigfoot I would love to
connect with you and hear your story!
If you enjoyed my book please join my email list by
visiting: www.chrisbossy.com
I promise not to bombard you with a thousand
emails but only important updates!
Keep it Squatchy!

If you enjoyed *Bigfoot Brothers*, keep reading for a preview of the forthcoming Bigfoot Brothers' prequel

If you enjoyed reading *Bigfoot Brothers*, turn the page for a preview of the forthcoming Bigfoot Brothers' prequel:

GOLD DIGGERS!

A Sasquatch Attack Survival Story!
Copyright © 2022 by Chris Bossy

scheduled for release in the second half of 2022!

To stay updated on the release date go to: www.chrisbossy.com and join the email list.

No GREAT WARS EVER start out thoughtlessly, but sometimes friendships do. Joe had come to the dump to go shopping and the dump didn't disappoint. His wooden cart was full of a six-foot piece of rain gutter and a ratty pair of stained wool pants. *Now I just need some kind of screens,* he thought. As he came around the corner he saw a skinny metal cage with two rats in it, in the hands of a tall tan-skinned boy with long jet black hair.

"Hey, that cage is exactly what I need!"

The boy stared at Joe a second, shrugged silently, and turned to walk off with the cage.

Joe yelled, "Wait, I said I need that! I'll pay you!"

The tan boy stopped in his tracks and half-turned to look back at Joe with an inquisitive look.

"I'll pay you after I sluice the gold from Phlegm Creek," answered Joe.

The tan boy laughed and jerked his head back and forth one-time and turned to walk off.

Joe yelled, "STOP," but the boy kept walking.

Joe grabbed a handfull of rotten purple olives from a huge olive pile on the ground and threw them like buckshot at the boy's back. They hit their mark, and the boy dropped the cage on the ground as his hands grabbed toward the stinging pain enflaming his back. He turned glaring angrily at Joe and picked up the olives from the ground at his feet and started throwing them at Joe aiming for his head.

SPLAT! A purple missile hit Joe in the center of his chest staining his white t-shirt. Clutching his chest and howling in pain, he felt a bumpy welt rise up on his skin. He dove toward the pile of purple ammunition grabbing two handfuls of mushy purple bullets and rose up to throw them right as another olive missile hit him in the side of the neck... another welt erupted. He screamed in pain and threw what was in his hands as hard as he could. The tan boy ducked behind a large pile of garbage, but not before a purple bullet hit him in the ear. Joe grabbed another handful of olives and jumped behind a pile of scrap metal.

"Give me the cage and you can go!" yelled Joe.

"This cage belongs to Chief Eagle Horse, not a scrawny pale skinned thief!" came the reply.

Joe poked his head around a jagged piece of steal, "I ain't stealing it, I'm just tryin to convince you to let me help you out Chief!" TING! an olive splatted on the metal next to Joe's head splattering purple juice onto his face.

"I don't want the pale-man's help for anything! Now stop bothering me, or else!" yelled the Chief. That's when they came around the corner and grabbed him.

"WHat are you doing here injun? Why aren't you at the Indian boarding school where you belong?" The Chief was squirming to free himself but it was no use. There were two of them. They were big boys that were almost full-grown men. No match for a thirteen-year old boy, even if he was tall for his age. One of them twisted the Chief's arms behind his back while the other one punched the Chief's stomach twice. The one holding the Chief's arms felt the Chief's lungs deflate and threw him to the ground hard. They bent over the Chief and started raining down punches.

Joe looked on from behind the pile of scrap metal. He recognized the boys and he knew they were real trouble. They had beat him up before, taking his lunch at school and ripping his only good shirt. They were the Klenchy boys. One of them pulled out a pocket knife and sneered laughing, "Let's scalp him!"

Joe moved quickly, grabbing two big handfuls of olives dropping them in his pants pockets as he moved toward the cage on the ground. He got to it and opened the trap door and reached in grabbing the rats by the tails. He had to hurry the Chief was screaming. He ran up behind the Klenchy boys and put a rat down one's shirt and one down the other one's pants. Then he reached in his pockets and started pelting them with hard purple olive bullets as he maneuvered around to stand between the Klenchys and the Chief. He glanced down at the Chief and winked as his reached in his pocket and dropped a handful of olives on the ground. The Chief grabbed some olives and stood up and began throwing the little bullets harder than he ever threw anything in his life. The Klenchy boys were covered in welts and purple stains before they knew what was happening. They stumbled and ran in terror trying to shake the rats out of their clothes, while screaming in pain as olives dented their epidermis causing welts to set their bodies on fire in too many places to count.

Joe yelled, "Leave my friend alone!"

The Chief looked at Joe then back at the Klenchy boys. He shrugged and smiled as he threw a few more olives at the fleeing targets. The Klenchy boys ran away and they didn't look back.

"Oh boy, did you see the look on their faces when I dropped those rats in their clothes?" exclaimed Joe.

The Chief asked, "Why did you help me? Everyone in this town hates Indians?"

"Guys like us gotta stick together or the Klenchy boys of the world will kill us!" said Joe proudly.

"What do you mean, 'Guys like us'?"

"You know, crazy guys like us!" said Joe.

"I'm Chief Eagle-horse! I'm not crazy!" protested the Chief.

"Well that's fine Chief," said Joe... "I'm crazy enough for the both of us! Just call me, "Crazy Joe"."

"Crazy Joe, I just have one question for you since you let my rats go. What am I going to eat for dinner now?"

"Oh don't you worry," said Joe confidently, "come with me to Phlegm Creek and I will buy you dinner!"

"I've never heard of Plegm Creek before, where is that?"

"You know that little bridge over the creek that runs through the woods behind the baseball field?" asked Crazy Joe.

The Chief cocked his head to the side and said, "You mean Birch Creek?"

Crazy Joe's eyes twinkled as he asked, "Chief, what do all the boys in town do when they walk over that bridge?"

The Chief smiled slowly, "They spit off the bridge into the creek."

"Exactly!" beamed Joe, "Phlegm Creek!"

"You are crazy!" said the Chief with a straight face.

"Maybe so Chief, but at least I don't eat rats for dinner!" said Joe smiling.

"Indians hunt and trap for their food," said Chief proudly.

"Well you can buy you some pet store rats for your dinner after we get all the gold out of Phlegm Creek," said Joe.

"Hmmm," hummed the Chief, "with a name like Phlegm Creek, I'm pretty sure the only nuggets we get out of there are going to be green not gold."

His bat was dragging as he walked down the trail with tears streaming down his dirt covered face. All he wanted to do was play baseball but they wouldn't even let him try out for the team. The coach's words echoed in his mind, "If you ain't tall enough for T-ball you can't play baseball!" The other kid's started laughing and commenting as he walked by the dug-out to leave the field.

"The bat is taller than him!"

"Does he get his clothes at the carnival?"

"He's a little leprechaun! Where is your gold little guy?"

He turned towards them red-faced and snapped! He swung his bat as hard as he could hitting the fence and barely missing a kid's fingers. The chain link fence rattled and the whole team spilled out of the dug-out like angry bees. He ran for his life. The coach yelled, "Get him!" He was short and stalky but he was fast. By the time he made it into the tree-line past center field, the mob pursuing him was barely passing second base. As he ran into the trees, he heard the coach's whistle let out a shrill scream followed by the coach's gravelly voice, "Okay! Okay! That little weiner-dog is gone, let's get back to work big dogs!"

THE RAIN GUTTER LAID on the damp ground at the water's edge. The rough wool fabric from the pant leg had been cut into long rectangular strips. The fabric lined the bottom of the rain gutter. The animal cage had been disassembled. The four mesh metal sides of the cage were each laid flat on top of the wool fabric in the rain gutter. Crazy Joe crouched down and announced, "The sluice box is built. Now all we need to do is lay this in the creek at the right angle, scoop material into the upstream end of it, and let the water carry the dirt over the ripples that will catch all the gold that is trapped in the dirt."

THWACK! THWACK! THWACK! echoed from atop the bridge. Crazy Joe looked at Chief. The Chief was pointing up to the bridge with three fingers. He looked at Crazy Joe and motioned for him to stay low and follow him up the bank through the bushes to see who was on the bridge. THWACK! THWACK! THWACK! THWACK! The Chief and Crazy Joe separated some bushes and peered toward the noise.

"I can hit harder than any of those fools!" THWACK! He crashed the bat against the railing. "I could hit homeruns!" THWACK! THWACK! The railing cracked.

Crazy Joe stood up straight and said, "Whoa! Easy does it slugger! There ain't no baseballs here!"

The boy spun around startled and raised his bat taking a step toward the bushes. The Cheif stood up to his full height and shook his head no.

The boy stopped and stepped backward, screamed and swung his bat cracking the railing with all his might. THWACK! THWACK! The railing exploded into pieces.

Crazy Joe started applauding. "Clap Chief." The Chief shrugged and started clapping. The boy with the bat looked up confused at the Chief and Crazy Joe clapping. Crazy Joe yelled, "HIT IT AGAIN!"

The boy wiped the tears from his cheeks and spit on his hands as he regripped his bat then he wound up and... THWACK! more of the railing splintered.

"YEAH!" yelled Crazy Joe clapping harder. The Chief raised his hands above his head clapping.

Encouraged, the boy wound up again... THWACK! A bridge post went flying into the creek.

Crazy Joe stepped out of the bushes and walked toward the boy with his hand out, "Wow! I've never seen anybody swing a bat like that in my life! I wanna shake your hand." The boy smiled and stuck his hand out. "What's your name kid?" asked Crazy Joe.

"Johnny" came the reply.

"I'm Crazy Joe. Hey Chief, come over here and meet my new friend, Homerun Johnny!" The Chief stepped onto the bridge and nodded to Homerun Johnny. "Listen Homerun Johnny, me and the Chief here are partners in a gold mining operation and we could use another partner. Do you want to be rich?"

"Sure I do!" said Johnny.

"Come with us," said Crazy Joe as he turned and led the way through the bushes and back down to the creek.

"Homerun Johnny your job is to use that bat to loosen up the dirt and rocks on this hillside." instructed Crazy Joe. "Chief, your job is to take Homerun Johnny's hat and fill it with the loose dirt and rocks and bring it to me. I will pour the dirt from the hat into the sluice box. Everybody has a job, let's get to work."

After an hour it was starting to get dark and Homerun Johnny announced, "I've got to get home guys."

Crazy Joe said, "I will take the sluice box home and clean it up and see how much gold we got."

"What about my dinner rats?" asked the Chief.

Homerun Johnny said, "Dinner rats?"

"It's a long story Homerun Johnny, but basically I promised the Chief enough gold to buy him two rats for dinner," explained Crazy Joe.

Homerun Johnny said, "I have lots of rats at my house! I see them in the chicken coop every day. You can have them all if you can catch them."

"Don't worry, I can catch them," assured the Chief.

Crazy Joe said, "Great! Chief you go with Homerun Johnny and I'll go home and work on the gold. Let's meet back here tomorrow morning and we'll split up the gold."

Homerun Johnny put his soil stained hat on his head and his bat over his shoulder and said, "Come on Chief!"

Crazy Joe watched them walk away and then picked up the sluice box and carried it up the hill to his wooden cart. He started started whistling and began his journey home.

JUST AFTER DAYLIGHT, JOHNNY went to the chicken coop to collect eggs for his breakfast. When he opened the creaky door, he found the Chief asleep in the corner of the chicken coop with a chicken nesting in his lap. "Did you get any rats?" asked Johnny waking him up. The Chief looked up bleary-eyed and held up a potatoe sack and gave it a little shake. Squeaks came from inside the bag. "Want some eggs for breakfast?" asked Johnny

"Sure!" said the Chief. He reached under the chicken on his lap and retrieved an egg. The chicken registered her protest with a squawk and hopped off his lap. Holding the egg above his face, he pushed into the shell with his thumbs cracking it open letting the gooey yoke drain into his open mouth. He tossed the eggshells to the ground, wiped his mouth with the back of his hand and said, "Thanks Homerun Johnny!"

"That's just gross Chief! You didn't have to do that, I'll cook you some eggs," said Johnny.

"Indians don't cook wild bird eggs, we drink them," explained the Chief.

"Well, I'm going to cook my breakfast! Come on inside the house."

The Chief grabbed a long red chicken feather off the ground as he got up and picked up his rat sack. While Johnny ate some fried eggs the Chief used a small strip of cloth he tore off his red shirt to tie the feather onto the braid in his black hair. Johnny's mom stared at the Chief suspiciously the whole time. Johnny quickly washed his plate and fork and said, "Let's go Chief!" Johnny grabbed his dirty baseball hat and bat from next to the kitchen door and exited with purpose. The Chief was following close behind him. "Sorry about my mom," said Johnny apologetically.

The Chief stopped walking and said, "My rats!" Turning quickly, he ran back in the kitchen door. Johnny's mom had the Chief's potatoe sack in her hands when the Chief entered the kitchen. "Don't look in there!" warned the Chief.

"Why? Did you steal something from me you dirty Indian?" she said glaring at the Chief. Defiantly she opened the sack and looked inside. A rat jumped on the back of her hand and ran up her arm before it jumped off and landed on the kitchen table. Johnny's mom screamed and feinted. Johnny came running back in the kitchen door and saw his mom passed out on the ground with the potatoe sack on the floor next to her. Johnny said, "Quick! We have to get out of here before she wakes up or she'll call the cops on you and I'll get a whippin."

"No cops," said the Chief emotionally, "they'll send me back to the boarding school!" The Chief grabbed the rat by the tail lifting it off the table and put it back in the rat-sack and ran out the door.

Johnny followed after him yelling, "Let's take my bike."

The Chief had never ridden on a bike before, so Johnny drove while the Chief stood on the foot pegs on the back tire. The Chief held the bat and the rat-sack in one hand and held on to Johnny's shoulder with his other hand. In ten minutes they were at the Phlegm Creek bridge.

When they pulled up they saw a shirtless Crazy Joe surrounded by four players from the baseball team. They were throwing Joe's balled-up t-shirt back and forth between them chanting, "bird-chest! bird-chest! bird-chest!" Crazy Joe was trying to jump up to grab his shirt everytime it flew over his head to another player. The Chief handed the bat and rat-sack to Johnny and walked determinedly toward the circle. He timed it just right and stepped inside the circle lifting his arm high into the sky catching the t-shirt mid-air. He handed it to Crazy Joe. A big blonde haired boy with a bat in his hand said, "Look an Indian! Are we gonna let a stinky Indian stop our fun?"

"Looks like he already did," quipped Crazy Joe. "Now run along before you get hurt." The Chief turned slightly trying to keep an eye on all of them at once. Crazy Joe was focused on the husky boy with the bat.

The blonde haired boy raised his bat and took a half-step forward, "I'll just crack you!"

Crazy Joe started laughing hysterically and shot a quick look at the Chief and winked. The Chief started laughing too and pointed at the boy.

"What's so funny?" asked the boy.

"You can't hit hard with that thing. Not as hard as Homerun Johnny!" answered Crazy Joe.

"Ha, I'm the best hitter in this whole town!" bragged the boy pompously.

Crazy Joe's blue eyes twinkled as he said slowly, "Wanna bet?"

The boy smiled and said, "Bet? Bet what?"

Crazy Joe said, "I bet Homerun Johnny can hit more homeruns in five minutes than you can!"

"Okay, I'll take that bet, but when I beat him what do I get?" asked the boy.

"If you beat Homerun Johnny, I'll give you our gold," said Crazy Joe as he reached in his pocket and pulled out a small glass babyfood jar with some gold nuggets in the bottom of it. "But if Homerun Johnny beats you we get your bat." said Crazy Joe.

The husky one said, "Deal! You go get this Homerun Johnny fella and meet us over at the baseball field."

Crazy Joe said, "No need, he's right there," pointing past the group to Homerun Johnny still sitting on his bike at the edge of the bridge.

The baseball players laughed. "Oh it's the midget from yesterday! This is going to be like taking candy from a baby! A tiny baby!" said the mean husky blonde haired boy. The baseball players marched off toward the field. The husky blonde one turned back and threatened, "If you don't show up you're all dead meat!"

When they were out of sight, Homerun Johnny turned red-faced to Crazy Joe, "What do you think you're doing volunteering me?"

Crazy Joe said, "I was trying to keep from getting beat up by those brainless muscle bags. Did you see how big those guys were?"

"Yes, they chased me off the baseball field yesterday. Why do you think I was destroying this bridge?" asked Homerun Johnny.

Crazy Joe reasoned, "Look we were about to get beat up, at least now we have a chance to escape unscathed."

The Chief asked, "Homerun Johnny how good are you at hitting baseballs?"

Homerun Johnny's lip quivered as he said, "I don't know, I've only practiced with a tennis ball."

The Chief groaned. Crazy Joe stuck out his bony chest and said confidently, "Don't worry boys! No matter what happens, I give you my word, we'll come out winners in this deal! Let's go."

Thank you so much for reading Bigfoot Brothers!
Please do me a huge favor and take a few seconds
to rate it and leave an honest review on the online
store or stores of your choice that carry my book.
I would love to hear from you!
Email me at: info@chrisbossy.com

If you have encountered bigfoot I would love to
connect with you and hear your story!

If you enjoyed my book please join my email list by
visiting: www.chrisbossy.com
I promise not to bombard you with a thousand
emails but only important updates!
I appreciate you!
Keep it Squatchy!

Acknowledgments

I would like to acknowledge; my wife: Mitzi, son: Walker and In-Laws: Joe & Loy Creel, who have allowed me to spend time in my imaginary world creating characters and stories during years of vacations and holidays. I would like to acknowledge and honor Bill Yeomans and Joe Creel. These two amazing men's feisty personalities and spirits inspired the Crazy Joe character. I would be remiss if I did not mention William Andrews who gave me permission to use the name Billy for the fictitious character Billy Anderson, whose endearing personality traits and characteristics were inspired by William Andrews. Author bio photo credit to Chesi McFadden of Chelsimcfadden.com. Cover art credit to 100covers.com

CHRIS BOSSY IS A Fort Bragg, California resident who has discovered that having an active imagination and hunting for bigfoot in the woods at night is terrifying and exhilarating. The earliest nightmare he can remember happened when he was six years old after a babysitter let him watch a King Kong movie that had a red hairy King Kong. That terror fueled his mind for bigfoot.

Bossy has been on a quest looking for bigfoot since he saw bigfoot images on television shows in the 70's. Thinking about bigfoot, talking about bigfoot, and looking for bigfoot is his favorite pastime. He is the lead pastor at a Baptist church, a High School tennis coach and an author. He has loved stories his whole life and dreamed of writing novels since he was in High School. Now he is combining his love of stories and his passion for bigfoot to create entertaining and encouraging novels. A weird fact about Bossy is that he is afraid of sloths! Connect with Chris by emailing: info@chrisbossy.com. Join Chris Bossy's email list and see what is ahead: www.chrisbossy.com

www.ingramcontent.com/pod-product-compliance
Lightning Source LLC
Chambersburg PA
CBHW031628200726

48288CB00019B/359